A

SPECIAL MESSAGE TO READERS

This book is published under the auspices of

THE ULVERSCROFT FOUNDATION

(registered charity No. 264873 UK)

Established in 1972 to provide funds for research, diagnosis and treatment of eye diseases. Examples of contributions made are: —

A Children's Assessment Unit at Moorfield's Hospital, London.

•

Twin operating theatres at the Western Ophthalmic Hospital, London.

•

A Chair of Ophthalmology at the Royal Australian College of Ophthalmologists.

•

The Ulverscroft Children's Eye Unit at the Great Ormond Street Hospital For Sick Children, London.

You can help further the work of the Foundation by making a donation or leaving a legacy. Every contribution, no matter how small, is received with gratitude. Please write for details to:

THE ULVERSCROFT FOUNDATION,
The Green, Bradgate Road, Anstey,
Leicester LE7 7FU, England.
Telephone: (0116) 236 4325

In Australia write to:
THE ULVERSCROFT FOUNDATION,
c/o The Royal Australian and New Zealand College of Ophthalmologists,
94-98 Chalmers Street, Surry Hills,
N.S.W. 2010, Australia

TRAIL OF THE HANGED MAN

Haunted by a missing past, Ben Lawless heads for Arizona to start a new life. On the way he provokes Joey Morgan's wrathful vengeance when he prevents him from hanging Sheriff Tishman. Then he helps his neighbour, Ingrid Bjorkman, to fight Stillman Stadtlander, a ruthless cattle baron who wants her land. Lawless will do anything for the beautiful Ingrid. But this deadly conflict will begin a series of perilous events that will lead him to the man who hanged him . . .

Books by Steve Hayes
in the Linford Western Library:

GUN FOR REVENGE
VIVA GRINGO!
PACKING IRON
A COFFIN FOR SANTA ROSA

STEVE HAYES

TRAIL OF THE HANGED MAN

Complete and Unabridged

LINFORD
Leicester

First published in Great Britain in 2011 by
Robert Hale Limited
London

First Linford Edition
published 2012
by arrangement with
Robert Hale Limited
London

British Library CIP Data

Hayes, Steve.
Trail of the hanged man. - -
(Linford western library)
1. Western stories.
2. Large type books.
I. Title II. Series
823.9′2–dc23

ISBN 978–1–4448–1166–7

Published by
F. A. Thorpe (Publishing)
Anstey, Leicestershire

Set by Words & Graphics Ltd.
Anstey, Leicestershire
Printed and bound in Great Britain by
T. J. International Ltd., Padstow, Cornwall

This book is printed on acid-free paper

To Andrea,
With Love

BOOK ONE

1

It was not the first hanging he had ever witnessed.

Out on the range and in towns and pueblos all across the Southwest he had seen outlaws, rustlers, murderers and even two innocent men dangling from the end of a rope.

But this was different. This time the victim about to be hanged from the limb of a Rio Grande cottonwood was a sheriff.

From the crest of the ridge he'd just ridden over, Ben Lawless could see a tin star glinting on the lawman's black vest. What was equally unusual, the person about to whip the horse out from under the sheriff was a boy of no more than fourteen. Clad in old jeans and a sun-faded denim shirt, the cinnamon-haired, freckled youngster sat bareback on a piebald as if he had been born on it.

Lawless hesitated, wondering if he should interfere. Hell, he owed the law nothing. Truth was, he'd had many run-ins with sheriffs himself and over the years had become familiar with the insides of more jails than he cared to remember. But during those years he had also witnessed several lynchings and they always turned his stomach. And though there was no angry mob gathered about this sheriff, only a callow, grim-faced boy, it was still a necktie party and Lawless pulled his rifle from its scabbard, aimed quickly and fired.

At the same instant the youngster whipped the sheriff's horse on the rump with a stick. The horse lunged forward, leaving the sheriff dancing in mid-air — then the bullet cut the rope and the big lawman fell to the ground.

The startled boy whirled his pony around and looked in the direction of the shot. He saw a tall, whip-lean, dark-haired man astride a dust-caked grullo watching him from atop the ridge; a man whose face was hidden by the brim of his black, flat-crowned Stetson; a man who, despite the intense heat, had his shirt buttoned up around his neck; a man holding a well-oiled Winchester '73 from which smoke curled.

'Damn you to hell!' the boy said and yanked the revolver on his hip.

Lawless dived from the saddle and rolled behind a rock. 'Drop it,' he shouted. 'I don't want to have to shoot you.'

The boy fired twice, the bullets ricocheting off the rocks and whining past Lawless before vanishing into the desert.

'Son, I'm warning you for the last time: drop your iron.'

The boy answered by firing two more rounds. Both bullets missed Lawless but chipped flakes from the rocks close to his head.

Irked that the youngster wouldn't obey him, Lawless snapped off a shot.

The .44–.40 bullet knocked the 1874 Remington Army revolver from the startled boy's hand and it fell on the ground. Rising, Lawless levered in another round and covered him with the rifle. 'Either you're deaf, son, or just plain eager to die.'

'I ain't deaf,' said the boy. Leaping from the piebald, he dived for his gun.

Lawless continued firing, each bullet sending the old cedar-handled revolver spinning across the sun-baked dirt. As he fired he walked down the slope toward the boy — who, frustrated, finally stopped scrambling after his elusive six-gun. Defiant to the bone, he stood glaring at the tall man.

Lawless confronted him, more puzzled than angry. 'What the hell's wrong with you, boy? You so all-fired anxious to hang this hombre you're willing to die for it?'

'Why not? Way my life's going right now, dying don't seem so bad.'

Lawless saw a lot of himself in the rebellious boy and lowered his rifle. 'No matter how big your problem is, son, dying isn't the answer. Now get back on your pony and ride out of here.'

'What about my pistol?'

Lawless picked up the revolver, fired the last two rounds in the air and tossed the gun to the boy. 'Here. Now, ride.'

The boy grabbed the halter rope and swung up on to his horse. 'I told Sis they'd be hiring gunmen next. Now, maybe she'll believe me.' He kicked the piebald into a gallop and rode away.

'Much obliged to you, mister.'

Lawless turned and saw the sheriff was now sitting up. He had also removed the noose from around his neck and was no longer choking. But he was embarrassed by his predicament and tried to hide it behind a rueful grin.

'Reckon you're wondering how a young pup like him got the jump on me?'

'Crossed my mind,' Lawless admitted. He spoke softly, choosing his words carefully, in an educated, faint southern drawl that belied his grubby, trail-soiled appearance. Taking out the makings he calmly built a smoke, making no attempt to help the sheriff get up.

The lawman grasped the trunk of the cottonwood, locked his fingers together and with a painful grunt pulled himself to his feet. He stood there, wobbly-legged for a few moments, gingerly rubbing his neck where the rope burns showed.

'Young Joey, he was hiding among those rocks yonder.' He pointed at some broken boulders. 'Must've heard I was coming back from Deming today.' His voice was raspy and he had to clear his throat and spit before he could continue. 'Anyways, he caught me napping in the leather and got the drop on me afore I could drag my shooter. I figured he was going to gun me down cold. But I was wrong. He and his sister's hatred has gotten piled so high that just shooting me wasn't enough. They want to see me hang.'

'Maybe it has something to do with the gunmen you're hiring?'

The sheriff snorted disgustedly. 'Ain't a lick of truth to that, mister. I got me a good reliable deputy and I could round up a posse quicker than you can say deputize. Nah.' He scratched his shaggy mane of iron-gray hair. 'It's just a young'un's mind all twisted up with lies fed to him by his sister and their old man, when he was alive. No more, no less.'

Lawless spat out a stream of smoke but didn't say anything. He was as tall as the lawman but leaner and harder, and moved with the grace of an Indian fighter. There was nothing memorable about his angular face except for his eyes: they were the color of the desert and just as unforgiving. Life in the saddle had taught him to embrace loneliness and enjoy silence as only a loner can. It also taught him to trust no one, rely on no one, and be self-sufficient. It had taken years of discipline to learn these painful lessons. But once he had, it gave him a quiet, unshakeable confidence that made men think twice before bracing him.

'I'm Tishman,' the sheriff said, offering his hand. 'Buck Tishman — though most folks call me Tish.'

Lawless didn't respond. He stared at the sheriff, his stoic expression making it impossible to tell what he was thinking. Then, as if grudgingly coming to terms with himself, he shook the lawman's meaty, callused hand. But he said nothing.

Neither did the sheriff. He'd looked into the eyes of countless men in his life, many of them dangerous, some even deadly, but never had he felt as uneasy as he did now. It was like staring into the yellow eyes of a wolf, a wolf that knew it could kill him any time it wanted yet for some reason was letting him live.

But Sheriff Tishman had not survived as a lawman into his fifty-third year because he was reckless or a fool. Stroking one tip of his drooping gray mustache, he said cautiously, 'I didn't catch your name, mister.'

'Didn't give it.'

'Uh-*huh*.' The sheriff sighed, a long resigned sigh that seemed to come clear up from his boots. Then he cleared his throat again and gently massaged his bruised neck. 'Been my experience,' he said hoarsely, 'that when a fella don't tell you his name, he's most likely hiding something. You hiding something, *amigo*?'

'If I was,' Lawless said, 'you'd still be dangling from that rope.' He turned toward the ridge and whistled. The grullo tossed its long dark mane and obediently came trotting down the slope toward him.

The sheriff watched as the slate-gray horse stopped beside Lawless. 'You trained him good, mister. I admire that. Me, now, I don't have the patience to train a hog to eat.'

Lawless didn't say anything.

'He's in real fine condition, too.'

Again, Lawless didn't respond.

'I always say you can tell a lot about a man by the way he treats his horse.'

Lawless had heard enough. Tucking his rifle into its scabbard, he grasped the reins and stepped into the saddle. He mounted in one slow fluid motion, eyes never leaving the lawman, right hand poised above his Colt. It was a gun-fighter's mount, economic, deadly and full of controlled violence. Once in the saddle he looked down at the sheriff, said quietly, 'Name's Lawless. Ben Lawless.'

The sheriff frowned, trying to place the name. 'Sounds familiar.'

'It'll come to you,' Lawless said, adding: 'Be riding on now.'

'If you got no objections, I'll ride along with you.'

Lawless shrugged indifferently, tapped the grullo with his spurs and rode off.

Sheriff Tishman watched him go, his expression a mixture of curiosity and uneasiness. He then collected his horse, mounted and galloped after him.

2

The two rode in silence, knee-to-knee, for several miles. They rode at a slow mile-consuming lope, following the trail through ancient red-walled canyons and across the flat, yellow desert with its clumps of mesquite and ocotillo, the midday sun broiling their backs, the only sounds made by their horses' hoofs and their saddles creaking — along with an occasional screech from one of several red-tail hawks drifting on the thermals high overhead.

'Where you headed?' the sheriff finally asked him.

'Borega Springs.'

'And then?'

'West.'

'West, where?'

'Just west.'

'And I'll wager if I asked you where

you come from you'd say 'just east'?'

'Southeast.'

'Mexico?'

'Chihuahua.'

'*Pistolero*?'

'I'm not that good.'

'Sure you ain't. I mean any damn fool can cut a rope with one bullet from fifty maybe sixty yards off.'

'Any damn fool can make a lucky shot, too.'

'You don't look like no damn fool to me,' Sheriff Tishman said. 'And you don't look like a man who needs luck, neither.'

Lawless didn't say anything. But inwardly he was amused. He'd aimed at the branch from which the rope hung, hoping to break it, and instead hit the rope. But he saw no reason to admit that to the sheriff.

'Either way, mister, luck or skill, I owe you my life and — ' The lawman broke off as it suddenly came to him and snapped his fingers, exclaiming, 'Got it!'

He turned to Lawless to say something and realized he was looking into the muzzle of a Peacemaker. Startled, he raised his hands.

'Whoa, easy, *amigo* . . .'

Lawless, satisfied there was no threat, holstered his Colt .45 almost as swiftly as he'd drawn it.

The sheriff lowered his hands. 'Mite touchy, ain't you?'

'If you're going to ride with me,' Lawless said, 'don't be making any sudden moves. *Entienda*?'

'*Entienda*.' The sheriff whistled softly to himself, marveling at how fast Lawless had cleared leather. He'd seen all the top guns in his time — Clay Allison, Doc Holiday, John Wesley Hardin, Latigo Rawlins — but none seemed faster than the tall, quiet man riding beside him. Not wanting to provoke him but anxious to satisfy his curiosity, the sheriff put his hands on his saddle horn, where Lawless could see them, said: 'I don't like to pry, *amigo*, but are you kin of Will Lawless?'

'Cousin.'

The sheriff nodded, satisfied. 'I knew the name sounded familiar. Ever ride with him?'

'You asking me if I'm an outlaw?'

'That weren't my intention.'

'Is it your intention to arrest me if I say yes?'

'Hell, no.' The sheriff chuckled, bit off a plug of chaw and with his tongue wedged it against his cheek. 'I'm so slow on the draw you'd think I had molasses in my holster. Besides, you just saved my life. Be mighty churlish of me to pay you back by making you a guest of the county.'

They started up a steep rocky rise, both slowing their sweating mounts so as not to wear them out.

'I never ran across your cousin, Mr Lawless, but from all the rumors I've heard he was faster than summer lightning.'

Lawless didn't answer, hoping his silence would end the conversation.

'I also heard a rumor he was mean to

the core and that when he was drunk, which was mostly always, he'd shoot anyone he took a dislike to — including women, children and dogs.'

'You heard wrong.'

'How so?'

'Will doesn't need to be drunk to shoot anyone. He plain enjoys killing, drunk or sober.'

'Ah-*huh*.'

Again, Lawless hoped that would end the conversation.

'Ever hear what happened to him?'

'Didn't know anything did.'

'Rumor I heard . . . the *rurales* stretched his neck down in Sonora some place.'

They had reached the top of the rise. Lawless reined in his weary grullo and gave him a breather. 'For a man who doesn't like to pry,' he said wryly, 'you sure hear a lot of rumors.'

The big lawman grinned. 'Never said I didn't like to listen.'

Or talk, Lawless thought.

They rode down the other side of the

rise, between clumps of cholla and mesquite, and started across a flat expanse of scrubland that ended at the outskirts of Borega Springs.

Still two miles away, the sprawling mish-mash of adobe and plank buildings shimmered in the heatwaves. Originally a dirt-hole pueblo known as a haven for outlaws and border trash, the town, like so many towns in the Southwest, had become respectable upon the arrival of the Santa Fe railroad. But despite law and order and an honest, conscientious town council, Main Street remained sun-scorched dirt in summer and ankle-deep mud in winter, and there were permanent ruts in it caused by the now-bankrupt Barlow-Sanderson stage line.

'Ever been here before?' the sheriff asked as they rode along.

Lawless shook his head.

'Nice little town. Folks are right neighborly. Do anything for you. Fella could do a lot worse than settle here.'

'I'll remember that,' Lawless said, 'if I

don't like Arizona.'

Sheriff Tishman sighed like he'd been pushed into a corner. 'Lookit, mister, if you're dead set on riding west, reckon I should warn you that you'll be passing right by their spread.'

'Whose?'

'The Morgans — Joey and his sister, Violet.'

'Want me to give them your regards?'

'Only if you're anxious for a bellyful of buckshot.'

'That was a joke, Sheriff. Where's your sense of humor?'

'Reckon I lost it back there a'ways, mister, when young Joey looped that noose around my neck.'

They rode on in silence, their shirts black with sweat, their lathered horses laboring in the intense, windless New Mexico heat.

Seeing the frown on Lawless' weathered, stubble-darkened face, the sheriff said, 'I know what you're thinking, *amigo*. You're thinking I'm one of them corrupt lawmen in the pocket of a greedy banker trying to steal the Morgans' ranch.'

Lawless, thinking exactly that, didn't answer.

'Truth is I'm the farthest thing from it.'

'So that's not why the boy strung you up?'

'Hell, no. Well, maybe. Who knows? Hard to tell what either of 'em are thinking these days, them being so full of hate.'

'Must be tough on you, you being so warm-hearted and all.'

The sheriff grunted, immune to sarcasm, and spat tobacco juice at a lizard sunning itself on a rock.

'Fact is it does bother me some. I don't like folks hating me — for any reason. I pride myself on being an honest, simple, Sunday-sit-in-church citizen . . . a lawman trying to do what the good folks of Borega Springs pay me to do — keep the peace without ruffling too many feathers.'

'Warm-hearted *and* modest.'

The sheriff chuckled. 'You sure do know how to prod a man, mister.'

Lawless looked at him, cold-eyed. 'So you've never tried to drive the Morgans off their ranch?'

'Not in a month of Tuesdays — though the day's fast coming when I'll have to serve them with foreclosure papers.'

'They're being kicked off their property?'

'Dispossessed. It's all legal.'

'Legal doesn't always make it right.'

'True.'

Inwardly, Lawless boiled at the thought of anyone losing their land. But his expression remained calm; almost disinterested. 'When are you serving them?'

'Any day now. You're thinking it again,' the sheriff said, as he saw an angry glint in Lawless's eyes. 'But you couldn't be more wrong. It's the dead opposite in fact. The bank's bent over backwards to help them young'uns keep their land. Held off on calling in the note months after it was due and even assured all the storekeepers that the Morgans' credit was still good. Hell's fire, no sooner than they'd laid their father to rest, Mr Edfors — that's Brian Edfors, the fella who owns the bank — was kind enough to offer Miss Violet a loan so she could buy more livestock and hopefully turn things around. But no, rather than accept his help, she turned him down flat. On top of that Joey tried to shoot my deputy when he rode over there to tell them they had to vacate the ranch.'

Lawless shrugged. He knew all about land disputes. Too often they turned into bloody range wars, like in Lincoln County, involving him in months of senseless shootings and killings when all he wanted was to earn wages.

'Reckon you've done all you can, then,' he said.

'Seems like.' Sheriff Tishman spat again, drenching another lizard with tobacco juice. 'Sure wish I could figure out a happier ending though. Makes my heart bleed to think of Violet and Joey having no place to live.'

'Why would you give two damns for them?'

''Cause I'm their godfather. Surprised, huh?' he said as Lawless arched his eyebrows. 'Well, don't be. There was a time, back in '69, when their pa and me were partners in a saloon in Silver City. Marion — his wife — had just passed away with the fever and I helped raise them two pups. I never had no young'uns of my own, nor brothers or sisters. But I loved Violet and Joey like they was kin. They felt the same about me, too. All of us, we were just one big happy family.'

'And now they're trying to hang you,' Lawless said. 'Some happy family.'

'Go ahead, mock me all you want. I'm just doing my job.' The sheriff fingered the rope burns on his neck. 'I tell you, mister, having them turn on me, cuts deep, mighty deep. Why, sometimes I get so riled up just thinking about it, I can't sleep, can't eat — ' He paused as Lawless cupped his hand to his ear as if hearing a noise, then said, 'What is it? You hear something?'

'Violins.'

'Violins?'

'Playing hearts'n flowers.'

Sheriff Tishman got the message. He reddened and spoke no more until they reached town. By now it was growing dark and lights glowed in the windows of the hotels, stores and cantinas lining Main Street.

They reined up outside the small adobe-walled sheriff's office. The lawman asked Lawless if he was hungry. Lawless nodded. But before he ate, he said, he wanted to get his horse grained and watered.

'Livery stable's up the street on your right.' Sheriff Tishman pointed. 'And over there, next to Hinnerman's Mercantile, the Hotel Parker's got the best steaks in the county. Cleanest rooms, too, in case you're interested in resting up for the night.'

Lawless nodded his thanks and started to ride away.

'Hold it . . . '

Lawless reined up, hand warily dropping to his six-gun. 'Yeah?'

'All funnin' aside, I'm mighty grateful for what you done.'

'Enough for a favor?'

'Just ask.'

'Don't arrest Joey for trying to stretch your neck.'

'Why would you care about what happens to Joey?'

'He reminds me of someone.'

Sheriff Tishman frowned and absently rubbed at his neck. 'All right,' he said finally. 'Reckon I owe you that much. But that wipes the slate clean. From now on, *amigo*, we're even.'

'Just how I like it,' Lawless said. He kneed the grullo forward and the big, placid, amiable horse plodded toward Capshaw's Livery & Feed.

3

After turning the grullo over to the hostler, Lawless got a room at the Parker Hotel. It was as clean and comfortable as the sheriff had described. Freshly ironed sheets covered the bed, prints of Audubon's birds adorned the walls and as a special touch, there were pine cones in each drawer of the chest-of-drawers to add fragrance to the guests' clothes.

Atop the chest-of-drawers was a porcelain pitcher of water, basin, towel and soap. Stripping down, Lawless washed away the trail grime and reached for the towel.

With his shirt off, a permanent scar showed all around the base of his neck. It was a grim ugly reminder of a distant day he never wanted to forget and yet, as of now, could only partially remember. As he toweled himself dry, Lawless studied his reflection in the gilt-framed mirror above the chest-of-drawers. He fingered the lumpy twisted flesh, trying as he did to recall the events that had happened during the five or six hours prior to and after the hanging. But as usual his mind remained blank.

For the life of him he could not remember who had hanged him, or why — or how he had escaped. Yet strangely, buried somewhere deep in his senses, he could still feel that single, awful moment when the rope jerked tight . . . the noose crushing against his jugular . . . choking him until all went black.

The next thing he was aware of, it was some time during the night and he was riding across the moonlit Mexican scrubland toward the US border. His neck hurt and the flesh was red and swollen with rope burns. And the following morning when he crossed the border at Columbus, New Mexico, and spoke to the gate-guard his voice was so hoarse he didn't recognize it.

Those ten or twelve missing hours remained a mystery. And now, as always since the hanging, just thinking about it caused him to be gripped by an uncontrollable panic. He held on to the chest-of-drawers to steady himself and gulped in lungful after lungful of air until the panic went away and he could breathe normally again.

'Damn you,' he said through his teeth. 'Damn you whoever you are!'

Calming, he opened his saddle-bags and took out an old but clean gray linen shirt. Slipping into it, he buttoned it up to the collar so that the scar was no longer visible. Then, buckling on his gun-belt, he went downstairs to the dining room.

The owner's wife had once worked in a Harvey House. Like many Harvey girls she had married one of her customers, and then later persuaded him to buy the hotel. The waitresses were young, polite and attractive. They wore neat black uniforms with white cuffs. There were snowy linen table cloths and gleaming silverware from St Louis, red velvet drapes, a slow-twirling brass ceiling fan and windows clean enough to see folks walking past on the boardwalks.

Lawless ordered a steak, burned. It hung over the sides of the platter and came with peas and mashed potatoes smeared in gravy, biscuits and honey and a wedge of fresh-baked cinnamon-spiced apple pie. He emptied his plate and washed everything down with several cups of rich black coffee. Stuffed, he paid his bill, then bought two Mexican cigars from the desk clerk and found a comfortable chair in the lobby to smoke one of them. It left him with just enough to pay the hostler. But he didn't care. Besides his uncanny ability with a gun he was good with horses and from what he had heard there was plenty of work for a wrangler in Arizona and the border was no more than two days' ride from where he sat. If he could reach there without encountering any trouble, maybe he could begin life all over again.

Maybe.

He was not taking anything for granted.

Presently a man approached holding a straw skimmer. 'Excuse me . . .'

Lawless looked up through his exhaled smoke and saw a small, slim, fastidiously tidy man of forty in a tailored brown suit and polka-dotted brown bowtie smiling at him.

'Are you Mr Ben Lawless?'

'Who wants to know?'

'I'm Brian Edfors. I own the — '

'— bank. Yeah, I know.'

'May I join you for a moment?'

Lawless gave him a second, closer look. The banker had rust-colored hair, thinning at the temples, merry brown eyes and a deceptive, engaging smile under a bristly mustache. But despite his friendly demeanor, Lawless sensed an underlying arrogance lurking beneath the little man's cultured charm.

'Draw up a pew.'

'Thank you.' Edfors carefully set his straw hat on the table. Next he took out a lavender-scented white handkerchief, flicked cigar ash off the chair facing Lawless, hoisted his pants at the knees and sat. 'I just finished talking to the sheriff and I want to thank you — for myself and for everyone else in Borega Springs — for saving his life.'

'I just happened to be riding by.'

'And lucky for us you were. You did us all a huge favor, Mr Lawless. This town — indeed this whole county desperately needs good men like Buck Tishman. They're all too rare these days, and we count ourselves blessed to have him as our guardian of the peace.'

Lawless felt his stomach turn. Until Edfors joined him, he had been enjoying the evening. Now, thanks to the banker's gushing flattery, lavender toilet water and irritating meticulous ways, it was spoiled and all Lawless could hope for was that Edfors would leave and let him smoke his cigar in peaceful solitude.

As if reading his mind the banker stood up, shot his cuffs, checked his reflection in the window, adjusted his bowtie, turned to Lawless and smiled his well-mannered smile. 'Well, sir, I'll leave you to enjoy your cigar. Goodnight, Mr Lawless. It was a pleasure making your acquaintance. And again, thank you.' Collecting his skimmer Edfors returned the waves of two elderly guests walking past, spoke briefly to the desk clerk and minced out.

* * *

Alone, Lawless leaned back in his chair and tried to recapture the feeling of serene contentment that always came after a full belly followed by a fine cigar. But despite trying not to, he kept thinking about Joey and his sister being evicted from their ranch. It brought back distant, bitter memories of the aftermath of the Civil War that he had thought were buried too deep to remember. Angry with himself for being soft-hearted, he dropped his half-smoked cigar in the spittoon and went to the front desk to collect his key.

Earlier, when he'd paid for the room, the clerk had taken one look at his grimy clothes and two-week stubble and had barely been civil; now, he beamed and greeted Lawless like he was a visiting senator.

'May I say, sir, it is indeed a great pleasure to have you staying with us.' He handed Lawless his key and a sealed envelope, adding, 'If there's anything you need, sir, anything at all, you be sure to let me know right away.'

Lawless, wary of the clerk's turn-around, opened the envelope and saw there were bills inside. 'What's this?'

'Your money, sir — for your room, dinner and cigars.'

'I don't understand.'

'Mr Edfors feels the town owes you a great debt of gratitude. Said the least we could do was repay you by not charging you for anything.'

'That a fact?'

'Yessir. Now, is there anything else I can do for you?'

'Just this: tell Mr Edfors that I appreciate his generosity but can't accept it.' He dropped the envelope in front of the surprised clerk and headed for the stairs.

'But, sir . . . ' Dismayed, the clerk grabbed the envelope, ducked under the desk flap and chased after Lawless. 'W-Wait . . . please . . . Mr Lawless, I can't do that, sir — '

'Sure you can.'

'No, sir, you don't understand. Mr Edfors wouldn't like it if — '

'What Mr Edfors does or doesn't like is of no interest to me,' said Lawless. 'So be a good fella and do like I say. Savvy?' Without waiting for an answer, he started up the stairs.

4

His room was on the second floor at the end of a hallway that smelled of pine-scented disinfectant and stale cigars. As he approached the door he thought he heard a noise inside. His hand dropped to his six-gun and he listened intently. Silence — save for the muffled sounds of horses and wagons moving along Main Street.

He cautiously turned the doorknob. The door was still locked. He relaxed a little. Inserting the key, he opened the door and entered the room, only to stop in mid-step as he saw a figure silhouetted against the open window — a figure aiming a rifle at him.

'Shut the door,' another voice said.

Lawless turned and by the moonlight coming in through the window, saw a second figure seated on the bed.

'You heard her,' the figure with the

rifle said. 'Shut the damn door!'

Recognizing the voice as Joey's, Lawless obeyed.

'Now, reach for the stars.'

'Son, before you do something you'll regret — '

'I said — reach!'

Wryly amused by the boy's dime-novel patter, Lawless obeyed.

'Don't try nothing funny, mister, else I'll fill you full of lead.'

Before Lawless could say anything a match flared, the flame revealing a slender young woman lighting the kerosene lamp beside the bed. It was hard to tell her age, but he guessed she was between sixteen and eighteen. She was dressed like the boy and vaguely resembled him, her pretty oval face framed by long, coppery-gold hair.

'You must be Violet,' Lawless said.

She turned to him, gray-green eyes filled with disgust, at the same time telling her brother to, 'Get his gun, Joey.'

Lawless stood there, tolerantly, as

Joey snatched the Colt from its holster and stepped back.

'First a hanging and now robbery — you're having a busy day, son.'

'Shut up,' Joey said.

'We're not here to rob you,' Violet said.

'Then how come you broke into my room?'

'We didn't. The window was open.'

'Wrong. I closed it before I left.'

'Well, it wasn't locked and — '

'Quit wasting time, Sis,' Joey blurted. 'Tie him up while I keep him covered.'

'Give me your hands,' Violet said to Lawless.

'And if I don't, what're you going to do — shoot me?'

'If she won't,' Joey said, 'I sure as hell will. I mean it,' he warned, wagging the rifle at Lawless. 'I mean it sure as I put a noose around Sheriff Tishman's neck this afternoon.'

There was enough anger in his voice to convince Lawless that he might pull the trigger. Offering out his wrists, he let Violet tie them with sash cord.

'What next?' he said.

Violet opened the door and motioned with his gun for him to leave.

'Now you can add kidnapping to your crimes,' Lawless told Joey.

'Button it,' the boy said. Jamming the rifle in Lawless's back, he pushed him out the door.

They descended the back stairs and left the hotel without anyone seeing them. Though it was dark Lawless could see a dun with three white stockings standing next to Joey's piebald. Violet untied the horses and led the way along the unlighted alley past the rears of several stores until they came to the livery stable. There, she took a pencil stub and a piece of paper from her Levi's. 'Can you write, mister?'

'What do you want me to say?' Lawless said.

'Tell Mr Grubbs that it's OK for Joey to have your horse.'

'Better think this through carefully,'

Lawless advised. 'Stealing a man's horse will buy you a rope.'

'We're not stealing it,' Violet said. 'We're just making sure you ride on out of here — out of New Mexico, if we have to.'

'Then we're of one accord, miss. Come sunup I'm headed for Arizona. It's true,' he added as she looked dubious. 'Just ask the sheriff. He'll tell you.'

Too late he knew it was the wrong thing to say.

'I wouldn't believe anything that slimy snake said,' Violet snapped, 'if he swore on a wagonload of Bibles. Now' — she pushed the pencil into his hand and held out the pad — 'write what I said.'

'Only be a waste of time. Mr Grubbs won't agree to it. I haven't yet paid him.'

'Joey will pay him for you.'

'Wouldn't it be simpler all around if I — '

'It's a far piece to our spread,' Joey

said. 'But if you'd sooner wear your boots out walking, that's fine with us.'

It wasn't easy with his wrists bound, but Lawless managed to scribble the necessary words. Violet handed the note to her brother, who gave her Lawless's six-gun.

'Plug this coyote if he so much as blinks, Sis.'

Lawless couldn't help grinning.

'What's so funny, mister?'

'You, sonny. You've been reading too many *Wild West Weeklys*.'

Stung, Joey reversed his rifle, ready to slam Lawless with the butt.

Violet quickly stepped between them. 'No, Joey! Stop it! Just get his horse.' Then as her brother defied her, rifle still raised: 'Don't mess with me, Joey Morgan. I'm not in the mood.'

He knew better than to push her. Wilting, he lowered the rifle. Then not wanting Lawless to think he was intimidated, he swaggered off into the stable.

Violet gave a troubled, motherly sigh.

'He's a handful all right,' Lawless agreed.

She immediately became defensive. 'My brother's really not like that, Mr Lawless. You can ask anybody. They'll tell you. Before Pa was killed Joey was a sweet, happy, good-hearted boy. Polite and well-mannered, too.'

'I doubt if the sheriff would agree with you.'

'Buck Tishman,' she said disgustedly. 'Fine excuse for a lawman he is. He might wear a star but he's nothing more than Bria — Mr Edfors' puppet.'

'Way he tells it, miss, he's just trying to do his job.'

'And of course you believed him! Well, I'm not surprised. How much is he paying you anyway — or did you get hired by Mr Edfors?'

'Nobody's paying me anything — least all that sugary, lavender-scented dude.'

'Then why are you siding with them?'

'I'm not. Not siding with anybody. I'm no shootist. I break broomtails for a living. You can believe that or not,' Lawless said as Violet looked doubtful, 'makes no difference to me. Like I told you, I'll be gone come sunup and then you folks can go on feuding for as long you please.'

She studied him with the widest, most honest eyes he'd ever seen. 'Just happened to be riding through — that what you're saying?'

She took his silence to mean yes.

'Then why'd you chase off my brother?'

'I don't like necktie parties.'

'Joey never meant to hang the sheriff. He just meant to throw a scare into him so he'd think twice before siding with Mr Edfors. Said the sheriff's horse got spooked when it saw you coming.'

'Ah.'

'You don't believe that?'

'I saw what I saw.'

She frowned, troubled by his sincerity. 'What exactly did you see?'

'Ask your brother.'

'I did.'

'Ask him again.'
'Very well. But — ' She broke off as Joey returned, leading the leggy, saddled grullo.
'Mount up,' he told Lawless.
'Well?' Lawless said to Violet.
'Well, what?' Joey said.
'Tell me again how it happened,' Violet said, 'the hanging, I mean?'
For an instant Lawless glimpsed uneasiness in Joey's eyes. Then it vanished and he grinned, almost cocky. 'I got the jump on that big toad and — '
'No, no, later. Why his horse got spooked.'
Again, uneasiness narrowed Joey's blue eyes. 'On account of seeing him,' he said, nodding at Lawless.
'You mean, when I was riding along the ridge?'
'Yeah.'
'Not later, while I was sitting there, watching you from the saddle?'
'No. I mean, maybe. I don't remember.'

'But you do remember me spooking the sheriff's horse?'

'Sure. I remember that, all right.'

'Even though you didn't see me until after I fired?'

'I saw you,' Joey lied. 'Just didn't pay you no mind.'

Lawless shot Joey a look that unsettled the boy.

'That's how it happened, Sis,' he blurted to Violet. 'And if he says different, then he's lying.'

'If I'm lying,' Lawless said, 'then the sheriff's horse has got eyes in its rump.'

'What do you mean?' Violet said.

'The ridge I was on, it's to the south-east — *behind* the horse.'

'Th-then it must've heard you,' Joey stammered.

'Would that be before or after you whipped him?'

'I never whupped him.'

'We can all ride back there,' Lawless said to Violet. 'I'll show you the stick he used. When the sheriff and I rode off it was still on the ground under the cottonwood where your brother dropped it.'

Joey began to bluster.

Violet cut him off. 'That's enough — '

'But it ain't true, Sis! I never whupped no horse! I swear. H-he's lying.'

'I said — that's enough!' Stepping close to Lawless, Violet untied the cord binding his wrists. 'I'm sorry, mister. Reckon I made a mistake.'

'Sorry doesn't cut it.'

'I don't know what else to say.'

'You can promise to keep your hothead brother, here, in tow. You don't, he'll grow up behind bars — maybe worse.'

'Damn you,' began Joey.

Lawless backhanded him, sending the boy sprawling. Stunned, he lay there, hand to his cheek, glaring at Lawless.

'Be glad I'm not your pa, son. I'd teach you not to damn a man or call him a liar.' He turned to Violet. 'He does either one after he starts shaving and you'll be burying him feet up.' Mounting, he nudged the grullo in the direction of the hotel.

'Damn him,' Joey said. 'I should've shot him when I had the chance.'

His sister angrily dragged him to his feet. 'You little fool! You should be grateful to him for not shooting *you* when *he* had the chance.'

'You throwing in with him now?'

'This isn't about taking sides. This is about right and wrong. And you're wrong. Wrong for what you did to Sheriff Tishman, wrong for lying to me about it, wrong for calling this man a gunfighter, wrong for — for — well, just about everything. And I only wish Pa was alive so he could pound some sense into you. You need it. Now, get on your horse and let's go home.' She stepped into the saddle and waited until her brother grudgingly mounted. Then, together they rode out of the alley, out of town, into the cold, silent desert.

5

The next morning, in the dewy gray light before dawn, Sheriff Tishman entered the livery barn and found Lawless saddling the grullo.

''Morning.'

''Morning.'

'Glad I caught you afore you left.'

Instinctively, Lawless' right hand dropped to his Colt. 'Something wrong, Sheriff?'

'Uh-uh. Just wanted to talk to you, is all.'

'I'm listening.'

'I talk better over breakfast, *amigo*.'

Lawless' stomach growled, reminding him that he hadn't eaten. With a shrug, he followed the lawman across the street to Millie's Eats.

The café was empty save for two gaunt, bearded desert riders, a bald Mexican cook and a hard, tight-lipped, sleepy-eyed waitress. Everything smelled of coffee, bacon and hot grease.

They sat at a plank table by a window overlooking the street. Lawless's survival instinct made sure he faced the door. The sheriff, sensing Lawless was broke, told the waitress to bring coffee and enough eats for four hungry cowboys.

'And your friend, what's he having?'

The sheriff laughed and fondly patted his belly, a belly that almost hid his large silver-and-turquoise belt buckle. 'Wonder how she knows I like to eat big,' he said, winking at Lawless.

They waded through platters of fried eggs, ham steaks, link sausages, and a mountain of hash browns then lit their smokes and sat back to enjoy their coffee.

Lawless kept waiting for the sheriff to say what was on his mind. But the lawman made no mention of it. Finally, with the sun now yellowing the rooftops of the buildings across the street, he could wait no longer. 'Let's have it,

Sheriff. I want to be halfway to Arizona by sundown.'

'Maybe after your hear me out, you won't need to go to Arizona.'

'I doubt that.'

The sheriff drained his coffee and leaned back, dug out a crumpled paper bag and offered it to Lawless. 'Lemon drop?'

Lawless shook his head. 'Just get to the meat.'

The sheriff popped a candy into his mouth, tucked the bag away and placed his huge fleshy hand palm-down on the table. For a moment he locked gazes with Lawless and then withdrew his hand to reveal a deputy star.

Lawless almost laughed. 'You aren't asking me to wear that, are you?'

'Why not? Fella handles a gun like you I want him beside me, not facing me.'

'Sorry.'

'Two hundred a month, room and board and free ammo.'

'That's more than fair, but no thanks.

I break broomtails, not people.'

'You expect me to believe that, *amigo*, after seeing you slap leather?'

'You better believe it,' Lawless said grimly. 'I don't like being called a liar.'

'Farthest thing from my mind,' Sheriff Tishman said. 'I'm just trying to take advantage of your skill with a gun. And to prove it, I'll up the offer from two to three hundred. Now, what d'you say?'

Lawless didn't say anything.

'Four?'

Lawless blinked. 'Four hundred a month?'

'And found.'

'Judas.'

'That mean you accept?'

Lawless ignored the question. 'Whom do I have to kill?'

The sheriff cocked his head, looking at him as if he were a rare artifact.

'I asked you a question, Sheriff.'

'Uh? Oh, yeah, sorry. It's just I ain't never heard anyone say 'whom' before. Mighty fancy.'

'I'll try to be more illiterate for you in future,' Lawless said. 'Now, answer my question.'

'Hopefully — no one.'

'Then why the high-roller wages?'

'I figure you're worth it.'

'You mean Mr Edfors does?'

Sheriff Tishman reddened, started to admonish Lawless, decided against it and swallowed, hard.

'Mr Edfors owns the bank, not the sheriff's office.'

'I've heard he owns both.'

'Then you heard wrong. Now, you ready to throw in with me or not?'

Lawless was tempted. Wear a star for twelve months and he'd have almost $5,000 — more greenbacks than he'd ever hoped to call his own.

'Tell you what,' the sheriff said, rising. 'I can see you're interested. So why don't you sit here a spell, think it over while you're finishing your coffee? And when you decide, stop by my office. I'll swear you in and then walk you over to your new digs. How's that sound?' Before Lawless could reply, the sheriff left money for the check, waved to the waitress and left.

Expressionless, she watched the lawman walk past the window and cross over to his office. She then brought the coffee pot to Lawless's table.

'How long you lived here?' he asked, as she refilled his cup.

'Nigh on three years.'

'Like it?'

'Better than some towns, worse than others. Why? You figuring on becoming a permanent customer?'

'With a deputy's badge.'

'Oh.'

'Would I be making a mistake?'

She held his wolfish, amber gaze without flinching. 'You don't look to me like a man who needs advice.'

'Didn't you ask around before taking this job?'

'Mister, I was so glad to escape from that hellhole cantina I was stuck in, this place seemed like heaven in a teacup.'

Lawless nodded, understanding. He'd held a few jobs he hated in the past. It wasn't fun. 'Guess I got my answer,' he said. Rising, he went to the door. There, as the waitress started clearing his table, a thought hit him and he looked back, said: 'By any chance, ma'am, do you know the Morgans?'

'Violet and Joey — sure. Knew their daddy, too. Good folks.'

'Then you'd vouch for them?'

'In a frog's wink.' Her gaze returned to the window in time to see the sheriff enter his office. 'Though it might not be the most popular vote in town, if you get my meaning?'

Lawless grinned, tipped his hat, opened the door and stepped out into the cool, windless morning.

* * *

Sheriff Tishman looked up from the stack of old wanted posters he was reading and grinned as Lawless entered. 'Have a seat,' he said, indicating the chair beside his desk. 'Coffee's heating up.'

'Thanks, but I intend to put some dust behind me.'

The lawman lost his smile. 'You ain't taking my offer?'

Lawless shook his head.

'That's too bad, *amigo*. I was looking forward to hearing more of them fancy words.'

'Maybe another time.'

'Sure. I can always use a good man. By the way' — the sheriff held up one of the Wanted posters — 'your cousin, Will — he's a dead ringer for you.'

''Cept for one thing,' Lawless said. 'He has a scar on his chest.'

'That'd be mighty hard to see if he kept his shirt buttoned all the time.'

'Nigh impossible, I'd say.'

The words hung in the air like a veiled threat, daring the sheriff to press the issue. Unfazed, the lawman swatted a fly that landed on the wanted posters and scooped its squashed remains into a waste basket.

'That's the problem with killing things,' he said pointedly. 'There's always a corpse to bury.'

'Beats getting buried yourself,' Lawless said.

'Never thought of it that way.' The sheriff shuffled through the posters, giving himself time to figure out how he could get his question answered without getting shot. 'This scar your cousin has,' he said finally, 'any idea how he got it?'

'Knife fight.'

'Where?'

'El Tecolote.'

' 'Mean that old cantina down in Las Palomas?

'Uh-huh. Got jumped by border trash.'

'You were there, then?'

'Heard about it later.'

'Self-defence, I bet.'

Lawless smiled mirthlessly. 'That was the 'rumor'.' He left.

Rising, Sheriff Tishman plodded to the doorway, stood there watching Lawless untie his grullo from the hitching rail. 'Rumor I heard,' he said, 'your cousin was piss-drunk and tried to carve up a soldier from Camp Furlong who was kissing his whore.'

'Wouldn't surprise me,' Lawless said. 'The camp's just a mile from the border and Columbus, across the railroad tracks, is a dry town.'

The sheriff chuckled. 'That's why I try never to ride south of Deming. In my book, folks who vote against liquor being sold don't deserve law and order.' He waited until Lawless had mounted before adding: 'That shirt of yourn . . . you always keep it buttoned up?'

'Winter and summer.'

'Must raise a powerful sweat riding in this heat.'

'Powerful.'

'Yet you still keep it buttoned?'

Lawless shrugged. 'Way I figure it, if the shirt-maker didn't want folks to use the top button he wouldn't have sewed it there.' Before the sheriff could question him further, he nudged the grullo into a trot and became part of the wagon and buggy traffic moving along the street.

Sheriff Tishman took a lemon drop from the bag in his vest pocket, put it in his mouth and sucked contentedly. The tart flavor soothed his tensions. Unhurried, he looked at the poster still in his hand. Above the words 'Wanted Dead or Alive — $5,000 Reward' Will Lawless's stubbled, mustachioed face glared at him. It bore a startling resemblance to the man riding away from him.

With a heavy sigh, the lawman re-entered his office and pinned the poster on the wall behind his desk.

He never wanted to forget that face.

As he studied it he absently fingered the rope burns on his neck, wondering as he did if the *rurales* really had hanged the Texas outlaw Will Lawless.

6

The Morgans' ranch was twenty miles from the Mexican border and a hard hour's ride west of Borega Springs. A thousand acres of open scrubland in an arid valley surrounded by canyons and steep rocky hills, its north-east property line bordered the little town of Santa Rosa while the south-east corner was occupied by a single level log-walled house, plank barn, bunkhouse, and several log-fenced corrals containing horses. There was a vegetable garden beside the house, fenced to keep out peccaries and wild deer. Beyond that was an old weathered wind-pump that towered above a stone-ledged well.

Lawless studied the ranch from a nearby rise. A herd of shorthorns grazed on the open scrubland. Mixed in with the cattle were several giant horses. Eighteen hands high, they were all bays with white stockings and distinct white feathering around their hoofs. Lawless recognized them as Clydesdales, a breed originating in Scotland, and wondered what they were doing in New Mexico. His gaze drifted to the east. In the distance, across seemingly endless miles of sun-scorched desert, Massacre Peak loomed up on the flat horizon.

Returning his attention to the house, Lawless glimpsed a flash of sunlight glinting off steel behind the nearest corral fence. Instantly, he dived from the saddle. As he hit the ground he heard a rifle shot. The grullo reared up with a shrill whinny, staggered forward on buckling legs and collapsed.

Lawless crawled to his horse. It breathed its last breath as he reached it. Silently cursing, he peered over the saddle and saw the same glint of steel momentarily appear then disappear behind the corral fence.

Easing his Winchester out of its scabbard, he leaned the barrel on the saddle, aimed at where he'd last seen the steel and waited. Shortly, the steely glint reappeared and after a few moments, a figure took its place.

Lawless squeezed the trigger. There was a painful cry and the figure pitched on its face. Lawless waited a few moments to see if anyone else appeared. When no one did he rose and hurried toward the corral. He had almost reached the gate when the door of the house opened and Violet came busting out. She leveled a 10-gauge shotgun at him.

'Hold it right there!'

Lawless stopped and raised his hands. 'Easy, ma'am.'

'Drop your gun,' she said.

'Your hand fired first. Shot my horse right out from under me.'

'You don't drop that rifle I swear I'll kill you.' She cocked both hammers.

Lawless dropped his Winchester. Without lowering his hands he thumbed in the direction of the body. 'Your man's over there. If you check his rifle, you'll find the barrel still warm.'

'You're wasting your breath,' Violet said. 'It can't be one of my men. They're off rounding up strays. There's just my brother and me — ' She broke off, horrified, as the truth dawned on her.

Running to the body, she saw who it was and gasped.

Lawless quickly joined her.

It was Joey all right — Joey with blood pumping from a hole in his chest.

Sobbing, Violet knelt and cradled her brother against her.

Lawless went cold. 'God help me,' he said. 'I didn't know it was him.'

'Liar!'

'I'm telling you the — '

'You gutless, murdering . . . ' She grabbed the shotgun and swung it toward Lawless.

He knocked the barrel aside just as she pulled both triggers. The shotgun went off with an ear-shattering roar.

Buckshot discharged inches from Lawless's head. Deafened, ears ringing, he tore the shotgun from her hands and tossed it aside.

She attacked him, fighting and scratching, pummeling him with her fists. He grabbed her wrists and held her, helpless. At the same time he spoke soothingly to her, trying to calm her. When that failed, he gripped her wrists with one hand and clipped her on the jaw. She slumped in his arms.

Lawless gently lowered her to the hot sand and turned to Joey.

The boy's eyes fluttered and Lawless realized he wasn't dead.

Yet.

Picking him up, Lawless quickly carried him into the house. A vase of wild sunflowers sat on a plank table. Lawless swept it off and gently set the boy down. He unbuttoned Joey's shirt and examined the wound. The bullet had entered his chest at an angle, just missing the heart. Turning Joey on to his right side, Lawless saw an exit hole under his left arm and felt relieved that he didn't have to probe around for the bullet.

Violet entered with an angry rush.

'He's alive,' Lawless said, 'barely.'

Her rage faded. 'Oh God, dear God,' she sobbed.

'Pull yourself together, girl. Your brother's going to need you.'

When she continued to sob, Lawless grasped her by the shoulders and shook her, hard. She snapped out of it and stood there, fighting shock.

'I'll r-ride into town,' she blurted, 'and fetch Dr Harlan.'

'By then Joey will have bled to death.'

'No! He can't! He mustn't!'

Lawless's grim silence seemed to stiffen her resolve.

'Mister, my brother's all I got and I'm not going to let him die.'

Lawless looked around and saw a wood-burning stove in the corner. Moving to it, he opened the furnace door and saw the embers were still glowing. 'Reckon I could cauterize his wound,' he said.

'You mean burn him?'

'He won't feel it.'

Violet hesitated.

'It's our best chance to stop the bleeding.'

'Do it,' she said.

'I can't promise it'll work.'

Violet thrust her tear-streaked face into his. 'You shot him, damn you. Now save him!'

* * *

They piled wood into the stove and made a roaring fire. Lawless then stuck the blade of his hunting knife into the flames and when it was white hot, he pressed the steel against the entry wound in Joey's chest. The stench of burning flesh as the wound sealed made Violet gag. But she hung in there, waiting while Lawless reheated the blade in the fire and then returned beside her. She then gently rolled her brother's limp, shirtless body on to his side and gritted her teeth as this time Lawless laid the white-hot steel over the still-bleeding exit hole.

Again the flesh sizzled. But this time the bleeding didn't stop.

'Hold him still,' Lawless told her.

While Violet held her brother on his right side, Lawless took a .45 cartridge from his gunbelt, gripped the lead between his teeth and pulled it from its brass case. He did the same with a second bullet. Then he poured the gunpowder from each case over Joey's exit wound, went to the stove and lit a long kitchen match.

'Don't watch,' he warned Violet. Without waiting to see if she turned away, he lit the gunpowder. It flared briefly and smoke curled up.

Violet retched, clamped her hands over her mouth and ran outside.

Lawless heard her vomiting. He took a swig from the whiskey bottle he'd found in the cupboard beside the iodine and bandages, and examined the wound. The blackened flesh had sealed, stopping the bleeding. He knew it might only be temporary but it was a good start. Uncorking the bottle of iodine he poured some over the wound before wrapping a bandage around Joey's chest and tying it behind his back.

When he was finished, he knew he'd at least given the boy a chance. Now it was up to a higher court whether he lived or not. Gently picking Joey up, Lawless carried him into the bedroom and placed him on the bed.

As he was covering the boy with a blanket, Violet joined him. She began to apologize for running out on him but he cut her off. 'Go heat up a big pot of coffee, strong as you can make it. We're going to need it before the day's over.'

* * *

They took turns sitting beside the bed, keeping alert with mug after mug of coffee, watching, waiting to see if Joey regained consciousness. He didn't. Day turned into night. Night turned into a chilling, misty gray dawn . . . and still the youngster lay as if dead.

'Is he going to die, you think?' Violet said.

'That's not for us to know,' Lawless said.

'He's in God's hands, that what you're saying?'

His silence answered her question.

She looked at her brother, carroty hair all tangled, eyes closed, face pale beneath his freckles, lying still as a corpse — and made a decision.

'Help me hitch up the team.'

'Bad idea,' Lawless said. 'Even if the ride into town doesn't kill him, which it most likely will, there's nothing more the doc can do — '

'We're not going into town,' Violet said. 'I'm taking Joey to my neighbors, the Bjorkmans. They're only a few miles south of here.'

'What can they do that we already haven't?'

'Take us to the Mescalero reservation. Ingrid's husband, Sven, knows the shaman, Almighty Sky — '

'Whoa,' Lawless said. 'Back up the wagon. You're pinning your hopes on an Injun medicine man? Goddammit, girl, you gone loco?'

'I don't know,' Violet said. 'Maybe. But according to the Bjorkmans — and other folks, too — there's a young girl on the reservation, a healer who supposedly has strange powers. There's some even claim she can bring back the dead. I don't know if it's true or not — it probably isn't — but right now, the way Joey is, it's worth a chance. Anything is to save his life.'

Lawless didn't believe a word of it, but he said anyway: 'I'll watch your brother. Ride over and ask your neighbors to bring the girl here.'

'They can't. She's sacred. Almighty Sky won't let her leave the reservation. He most likely won't let us see her either, not even if Mr Bjorkman asks him to. But I have to take that chance.

If I don't and Joey dies I'll . . . never forgive myself. Now,' she added crossly, 'you going to help me hitch the team or not?'

'Lead the way,' Lawless said.

7

While Violet cradled her unconscious, blanket-wrapped brother in the back of the wagon, Lawless kept the team at a smooth steady pace. The trail ran string-straight across the desert. It was barely wider than the wagon and full of pot-holes. But with the help of the morning light he avoided most of them and kept the wagon from bouncing around too much.

The Bjorkmans' ranch was only five miles to the south-west. It wasn't much — half of Greenwater Canyon and 300 acres on which sat a stout, two-bedroom log house next to a barn, corrals and an old windmill to pump water into the well. According to Violet, Sven Bjorkman worked at the survey-or's office in Santa Rosa. But his dream was to raise horses and sell them to the army stationed at Camp Furlong.

For the first few years surveyor work had been plentiful and it seemed like his dream would come true. But then lack of rations and supplies had driven many of the Apaches from the reservation. Hiding across the border in the Sierra Madre, their marauding bands had all but shut down surveying parties and now, as Lawless drove the wagon past the corrals, he saw they were empty and that the barn and fences needed repairing.

Ahead, the glow of a hurricane lamp showed in the window of the squat log-house. As Lawless reined up the team, the door opened and a man wearing patched working clothes and holding a scattergun, stepped out.

He was a big robust man, not as tall as Lawless but much broader and thicker in the chest. He had friendly blue eyes and a blunt cheerful face that was half-hidden by a blonde beard inherited from his Norsemen ancestors.

Not knowing Lawless, he quickly

leveled the shotgun at him. But on recognizing Violet, his distrust turned to concern. Lowering the shotgun he quickly asked her what was wrong.

Fighting tears, she explained that Joey had been shot. She didn't say who shot him, which surprised Lawless, but instead described her brother's condition and asked Sven to ride with them to the reservation to talk to Almighty Sky.

He looked puzzled. 'But Almighty Sky is a shaman — a shape-shifter who can supposedly predict the future — not a doctor.'

'I know that,' Violet said. 'But we need his permission to . . . to . . . ' Tears choked off her words.

Lawless leaned forward on the wagon seat until he was right in Sven Bjorkman's face. 'We brought Joey here, mister, because his sister thinks the only person who can save him is a Mescalero girl, some kind of healer who lives on the reservation. I don't know her name, but — '

'It's Lolotea,' a woman said, appearing in the doorway.

Lawless looked at her. She had dressed in a hurry, missing some of the buttons on her blue cotton dress. He guessed she was on the good side of thirty. She was everything he liked in a woman — small, shapely, with brave blue eyes, a mouth made for smiling and tawny sun-streaked hair pulled back in a bun. He found her wholesomely pretty yet at the same time genteel — a rare quality in this harsh desert country — and couldn't think why she'd settled here.

'Y-yes, that's her,' Violet said, sniffing back tears. 'Will you and Mr Bjorkman ride with us to the reservation? You're acquainted with Almighty Sky. Maybe if you asked him, he'd let her help Joey.'

'Go with them, dear,' Ingrid said as her husband hesitated. 'See what you can do.'

'Be glad to,' he said. 'But I can't promise anything, Violet. The Mescaleros have always been friendly toward us.

But it's not their nature to trust strangers. Nor have they ever let white men speak to Lolotea. They are afraid, I think, we might steal her gift.'

Lawless, who found it hard to take his eyes off the woman, said to Sven, 'More likely they're worried we'll find out she's a fraud.'

'She's no fraud,' Ingrid said. 'No one off the reservation knows what her powers are, but she definitely can heal people.'

Someone squeezed past her and stood looking up at Lawless. He saw it was a boy — no, a girl, no more than twelve, with short black hair as shiny as a crow's wing and big, expressive, black eyes.

'I seen her do it once,' she said.

'Hush, Raven,' Ingrid said.

'It's true, Momma. Two years ago Running Wolf's son, Lame Dog, was attacked by Comanches. They pinned him to a tree with a lance and left him for dead. The Apaches expected him to die. But Lolotea talked to the Spirit God and Lame Dog lived.'

'You *saw* him cured,' Lawless said doubtfully, 'or heard about it? Which is it, miss?'

'I saw it,' Raven said.

'You sure?'

'I said so, didn't I?' Seeing doubt lingering in his eyes, she added angrily, 'Can believe me or not, I don't care. Who are you, anyways?'

'Ra-*ven*!' Ingrid chided. 'Mind your manners.'

Raven ignored her. Grasping her father's hand, she glared defiantly at Lawless. 'You heard him, Pa. He good as called me a liar.'

'Hush,' Sven said gently but firmly. 'You know better than to speak that way to your elders. Now, go indoors.'

As if God had spoken, Raven obeyed without argument. Giving Lawless a final glare, she squeezed past her mother into the house.

'Please forgive her,' Sven said to Lawless. 'Raven doesn't mean to be rude. She's just set on speaking her mind.'

'No harm done,' Lawless said. 'But if you aim on taking us to the reservation, better saddle up.' He looked back at Joey, still unconscious in his sister's arms. 'I doubt the boy will hold on much longer.'

'I'll get my horse,' Sven said, and ran to the barn.

Ingrid looked long and hard at Lawless, trying to place him. 'I don't think I've seen you before.'

'No, ma'am. I'm just riding through.'

She nodded, understanding. 'It's a harsh and unforgiving land,' she said. 'I often wonder why anyone would not keep on riding.'

Huddled in the rear of the wagon Violet fought down her tears. 'I surely wish you'd come with us, Mrs Bjorkman. You *and* Raven. Then Almighty Sky couldn't refuse us.'

'Sven will be more than enough,' Ingrid assured. 'It's his family the Mescaleros respect, not mine. Sven's father, Johan, once saved Almighty Sky's life. From that day on the

Apaches have been our friends.' Seeing Violet's disappointment, she added, 'Tell you what: I'll fetch you some tobacco and coffee. Almighty Sky seldom gets any now that the Indian agent has cut their rations. It's little enough as treats go, but it might help persuade him to let you see Lolotea.' She hurried into the house.

Lawless leaned back against the wagon seat and watched her through the open door. He found her pleasing to look at. She crossed in front of the lamp, its glow turning her tawny hair gold. Back now to him, she took a can of coffee from the pantry. Opening it, she poured some into a smaller can, capped it and returned the first can to the shelf. She then took tobacco and cigarette papers from a drawer. His eyes never left her. She moved with uncommon grace, seemingly unaware of her sensuality, and he ached to put his arms around her.

The urge was so strong it surprised him.

He'd known a few women in his life, but none was the permanent kind. That was to be expected. He'd never stayed in one place long enough to even get to know the whores he'd bedded, let alone the names of women he considered worth marrying.

Besides, he'd always figured he would end up dying alone.

He wondered if it was too late to change; if he could find a woman like this one, to settle down and raise young'uns. There was still time. He wasn't sure exactly how old he was, but he knew he couldn't be more than thirty-five or forty. If he really wanted those things, all he had to do was ride back to Borega Springs and work steady for Sheriff Tishman —

He heard a mocking laugh. It interrupted his thinking, and when he looked around he realized the laugh had come from him.

Marry?

Settle down?

Raise young'uns?

Dream on, *hombre.*

A horse came galloping up. Lawless looked into the rider's honest face, a face full of strength and integrity — a face that promised a woman devotion and stability.

'Let's ride,' Sven Bjorkman said.

Lawless raised the reins, ready to slap the horses.

'Wait! Take this with you . . . ' Ingrid ran up to the wagon and offered him a small cloth bag containing coffee and tobacco.

Lawless took the bag, feeling as he did her small strong fingers trapped under his. It felt like he was holding sunshine. He didn't want to let go. But the love in her eyes was only for her husband and he grudgingly turned her hand loose.

'Thank you, ma'am.' He touched his hat politely.

Ingrid smiled and turned to her husband. 'Hurry back, dearest.'

Sven blew her a kiss and spurred away.

Lawless, knowing he would never hear those words, savagely whipped the team with the reins. The startled horses surged ahead, jolting everyone, dragging the wagon behind them.

'Not so fast!' Violet shouted. 'You'll start Joey bleeding again.'

Lawless tugged on the reins, slowing the team. He had never known jealousy before. The strange emotion caught him off-guard, leaving him embarrassed and disappointed in his behavior.

Apologizing to Violet, he silently vowed not to let it happen again.

8

A warm, gold-blue morning had chased the dawn away by the time they reached the Mescalero reservation. There were no signs or fences indicating where Indian land began, but one look at the barren, sun-scorched earth that rejected cultivation and was home to rattlers, scorpions and Gila monsters told Lawless they were now on the reservation.

Ahead, in a barren valley surrounded by bleached-white hills and towering sandstone cliffs, the main village stood alongside a shallow creek. The greenish, copper-tainted water moved sluggishly past a group of squaws scrubbing their clothes on some flat rocks. Others carried clay pots of water to their fires, where older women were boiling the water to make it fit for drinking. Squalor surrounded the cluster of grass-thatched, dome-shaped wickiups, most of which needed repairing. Grubby, half-naked children played in the dirt outside each doorway. Nearby, goats and dogs nosed amongst the litter for anything edible.

The sight depressed Lawless. He had no love for the Mescaleros, or Apaches in general. Over the years they had often ambushed him on both sides of the border and but for his accuracy with a rifle, would no doubt have lifted his scalp. But to see the once-proud nation dying a slow miserable death brought him no pleasure.

He looked away, disgusted, and saw a herd of gaunt ponies grazing on the scrubland not far from the Indian Agency. The log-walled house, with its living quarters in back, stood alone on higher ground. Presently, it was not open and a long line of old men and women stood waiting outside a closed door marked: Food — Supplies. They watched impassively as Sven rode past, followed by Lawless, Violet and Joey in the wagon.

Lawless met the gaze of several of the Apaches and saw nothing but defeat and humiliation in their dark solemn eyes. No wonder the braves keep breaking out, he thought compassionately. I'd sooner be a hunted renegade holed up in Chihuahua than stay here, half-starved and waiting to die.

When they reached the outskirts of the village they were confronted by two mounted reservation policemen. Former army scouts who had fought for General Crook against Geronimo, both had graduated from Carlisle Indian University and spoke flawless English.

The younger man, Charlie Horse Nose, blocked the wagon's path with his pony while the other, a fierce-eyed Apache of forty wearing a red head band and a blue cavalry tunic over his shirt and breechcloth, rode up to Sven and demanded to know why he'd brought strangers on to the reservation.

'These people are my friends,' Sven said. He indicated Joey, adding: 'This girl's brother is near death. We must see Almighty Sky immediately.'

'He is in council and cannot be disturbed,' the policeman said.

'Jim, for God's sake,' Sven said. 'It's urgent. The boy may die any moment. Please . . . take us to him.'

James Tall Tree looked first at Joey and then at Violet, who gave him an imploring look. 'Let them pass,' he told Charley Horse Nose.

The young policeman grudgingly backed his pony out of the path of the wagon.

James motioned for Sven to follow him, whirled his pinto around and led the way into the village.

* * *

Although they had seen Sven Bjorkman many times in the past, the presence of white strangers attracted a crowd of men, women and children. Emerging from their dwellings, they walked alongside the wagon, dark solemn eyes fixed on Lawless, Violet and Joey, their expressions a mixture of curiosity and resentment.

Shortly, James Tall Tree reined up outside the large council-and-ceremonial wickiup. Dismounting, he told Sven to wait and ducked inside.

Lawless tied the reins around the brake and went to jump off. But Sven signaled to him to remain on the wagon. It was considered impolite he explained, to dismount before they were invited.

They waited in silence, ignoring the sullen stares of the Apaches gathered around them.

Ten agonizingly slow minutes passed.

Lawless looked back at Violet, who still held Joey cuddled to her, and smiled reassuringly. She didn't respond. Cheeks wet with tears, she kept her face pressed against her brother's and continued to cry without sound.

Guilt ate at Lawless. Despite knowing he had reacted as any man would after having his horse shot out from under him, he could not shake the thought of killing a boy of fourteen. It was a nightmare he knew would haunt him to his grave and silently damned the day he had left Chihuahua and crossed the border into New Mexico.

Finally, James Tall Tree emerged from the council wickiup. Good news, he told Sven. Almighty Sky had agreed to talk to them after he was done 'making speak' with the Elders.

'How long's that going to take?' Lawless said.

The Apache policeman shrugged. 'You cannot rush wisdom, White Man.'

'Tell that to Joey's corpse,' Lawless said.

9

Almighty Sky's wickiup sat on the bank of the creek, closer to the water than the rest of the village. Despite his exalted position in the tribe, the shaman's wickiup was rundown like all the others. The jawbone of an elk, split in half and painted white with a gray eagle's feather attached to the rear, hung over the doorway — a doorway that faced east so that Almighty Sky would awaken each day with the first rays of the sun warming his face.

According to Apache superstition, anyone walking under the jawbone would be blessed with good luck. And those who touched it as they ducked under it and then spat on their fingertips would not only be lucky but would be able to pass their good fortune on to their descendants.

Lawless, who didn't believe in superstitions, Indian or white, ignored the jawbone and reined in the team outside the shaman's dwelling. Climbing into the back of the wagon, he gathered Joey in his arms and gently lowered the boy to Sven, who took him into the wickiup. Violet followed. Lawless jumped down, took out the makings and rolled a cigarette. Without asking, he tossed the makings to James Tall Tree, flared a match and lit both of their smokes.

The policeman nodded his thanks. Together the two sat on the bank and looked across the creek at the solitary wickiup built on the opposite shore. It was a sight rarely seen by Pale Eyes. Considered sacred, it was covered in white goose feathers painstakingly woven into the grasses and strips of yucca leaves. A white ceremonial blanket hung over the entrance above which dangled a string of ancient seashells that tinkled musically in the breeze. The wickiup gleamed like snow in the sunlight, reminding Lawless of a picture of an igloo he'd seen in a magazine in a barbershop in El Paso.

'Those two,' he said, pointing at the muscular young braves standing outside, 'are they Lolotea's guards?'

'The Sacred One does not need to be guarded by earthlings,' James Tall Tree said disdainfully. 'As her name implies, she is a 'Gift from the Great Spirit'. He watches over her at all times. Runs With Head Up and Walking Man are merely her shadows. She speaks to them by thought and they do as she asks without question.'

Lawless didn't say anything.

'I can tell by your eyes that you do not believe me.'

Lawless shrugged and flipped his butt into the creek. 'Let's just say I'm sceptical.'

* * *

The sun had climbed above the craggy pinkish-yellow cliffs by the time Almighty Sky arrived. By then Lawless and Sven were pacing outside the wickiup and Violet had grown frantic. Miraculously, Joey was still alive. But Lawless sensed by now the boy had lapsed into a permanent sleep.

The old shaman, a stooped, frail man whose leathery wrinkled face was framed by two long gray braids, greeted Sven cordially and led the two men into his wickiup.

Inside, there was room for six people to sit around the fire pit centered under the smoke hole in the roof. Almighty Sky sat cross-legged facing the door, an old blanket draped over his permanently hunched shoulders. He looked gravely at Joey, who lay inertly in his sister's arms.

He took forever to speak. He sat motionless, his lidded glittering eyes barely open, his breathing so slow and rhythmic Lawless wondered if he had drifted off. He glanced at Sven, who mouthed 'Patience' to him.

Finally, Almighty Sky broke his silence. 'It has been told to me in a vision,' he said to Violet, 'that your brother sleeps in a place where he hears no one.'

About to reply, Violet saw Sven shake his head and remained silent.

'It is also known to me that you have brought him here so the Sacred One may cure him.' He paused and sucked on his few remaining teeth, then turned to Sven and spoke in Mescalero. 'You are not one of those who wish to see all Apaches dead. These old ears will hear you when you speak. Can you tell me why I should allow this to happen?'

'No,' Sven replied in the same tongue. 'No more than I can tell you why many summers ago my father chose to save you from the Comanches. Long before he found you staked out over the ants, Apaches had murdered and scalped his sister, her husband and their two daughters. His hatred for all Indians was legendary.'

'I have heard this,' Almighty Sky said. 'And to this day his act of mercy still puzzles me.'

'These are mysteries only the Great Spirit can answer,' Sven said. 'They are too deep for mortals to understand.'

'This is true,' the old shaman agreed. Without pausing he added: 'Do you have tobacco for me?'

'I don't know what the hell you two are chewing on,' Lawless said to Sven, 'but in case it's slipped your mind, Joey's life is clinging to a straw.'

Sven ignored him. Turning to Violet, he told her to give Almighty Sky the coffee and tobacco that Ingrid had given her.

Violet obeyed.

Almighty Sky nodded his thanks, took out the tobacco and papers and with fumbling fingers 'made smoke'. Pulling deeply on the cigarette, he slowly exhaled a stream of smoke before saying: 'I will speak to the Sacred One.' Rising, he ducked out of the wickiup.

Sven smiled at Violet. 'I think your prayers have just been answered.

10

They hadn't long to wait.

Lawless barely had time to roll a cigarette before Almighty Sky re-entered the wickiup. Violet looked at him hopefully. He ignored her and sat there stoically staring at the dirt floor. Lawless studied him from across the fire pit but could not tell what he was thinking. Finally the old shaman looked up and spoke directly to Sven.

'*Nii nahii'maa at'e, ya nahiika'*ee *at'e* . . . '

'What'd he say?' Violet asked.

'The earth is our Mother, the sky is our Father.'

'What's that mean, Mr Bjorkman? Why did he say that?'

'He's reminding us that we and the universe are all one . . . in perfect harmony. And therefore what happens to Joey happens to all of us.'

'Tell him to quit the council fire lingo and talk English,' Lawless said to Sven. 'All this translating is taking seconds off the boy's life.'

Almighty Sky studied him tolerantly, eyes full of wisdom. 'I hear your words, Tall Man. But you are on my land, in my lodge, among my people. Should it not be you who speak my tongue?'

'I'd be happy to,' Lawless said. 'But I can't speak Apache.'

'And so it goes,' the old shaman sighed. 'We, The People, who have lived here for more than a thousand winters, must change, must give up our language, our ways, our life in order to survive in the Pale Eyes' world.'

'No one's saying that your people aren't being treated unfairly,' said Lawless. 'But right now the fate of the Apache isn't up for discussion. This is about Joey: it's his life that's on the line — '

'Mister, don't crowd him,' Sven began.

Lawless ignored him. 'So I ask you,

hombre a hombre,' he said to the shaman, 'is the Sacred One going to try and save Joey, or not?'

Almighty Sky looked offended. 'Impatience,' he said, 'is a white man's word.'

'So is decision,' Lawless said. 'And right now that's what you got to do — decide! Otherwise we need to start digging the boy's grave, because he's going to die just as surely as if you'd shot him full of arrows.'

Almighty Sky gave Lawless a warning stare. 'Be careful, Tall Man. Do not let guilt guide your anger.'

'What's he talking about?' Sven said.

'Somehow the old devil knows I shot Joey,' Lawless said. 'Thinks that's why I'm so anxious to save his life.'

'*You* shot Joey?' Sven said, shocked.

Lawless had already turned back to Almighty Sky. 'If you know I shot the boy, you must also know it was unintentional.'

'So does the Sacred One. And because of this, Tall Man, she has asked that it be you who brings the boy to her.'

Violet sagged with relief. 'Thank God,' she whispered. She started to thank Almighty Sky, but Sven waved her silent before she could offend the old shaman.

Lawless kneeled beside her, 'Here, let me have him,' gently grasped Joey in his arms and got to his feet.

Sven went to the door and raised the blanket so Lawless and Almighty Sky could duck under it. Violet started after them but Sven held her back.

'Why can't I go too?' she protested. 'Joey's my brother.'

'I know,' Sven said. 'But the Sacred One has spoken. And for now, we must do as she asks.'

* * *

Led by Almighty Sky, and watched by most of the village, Lawless waded across the creek with Joey in his arms. The brackish water reached up to his knees. He knew it must be cold but he didn't feel anything. He didn't hear anything either — other than his heart hammering in his chest. He glanced down at Joey's pale freckled face, at his closed eyes and slack-jawed mouth, and thought: Hang on, boy. Hang on for just a mite longer so Lolotea can bring you back to us.

'It is good, Tall Man.'

Lawless realized he had reached the other bank and that facing him was Almighty Sky, his lidded dark eyes bright with compassion.

'What is?'

'That you now believe in the Sacred One's powers.'

Lawless frowned, unable to figure out how the old Medicine Man had read his mind.

'If it'll help save Joey,' he said, 'I'll believe in the Devil himself.' Pushing past Almighty Sky, he carried the boy up the bank.

Ahead, Walking Man and Runs With Head Up stood blocking the entrance to the sacred white wickiup. Both watched Lawless approaching, eyes full of hatred and distrust.

He kept walking, Joey's limp body cradled in his arms. The Apaches' fierce expressions never changed. Lawless returned their stares, undaunted. He wondered if this was some kind of gauntlet that he had to survive in order to reach Lolotea, and regretted obeying Almighty Sky's order to leave his shooter with Sven. But at the last moment the two braves stepped aside.

Pausing, Lawless looked back to see if the shaman had any final instructions.

Almighty Sky stood at the water's edge, withered arms outstretched toward the sun. 'Enter,' he said. 'The Sacred One awaits you.'

Walking Man now lifted the white blanket covering the entrance and Lawless ducked inside.

The seashells, once buried under an ancient sea, tinkled musically behind him.

11

Once inside, Lawless was surprised to find the sacred wickiup devoid of all comforts and religious pretentiousness.

No bed of soft pelts to sleep on. No fire pit to cook over or to keep warm by in winter. No customary smoke hole in the roof. No idols to pray to. Not even the usual spiritual paraphernalia — sacred bones, teeth, beads, amulets — that Apache holy men used to read the thoughts of the Great Spirit.

Only a simple white blanket spread in the middle of the dirt floor.

On that blanket, legs tucked under her, sat the Sacred One.

Lawless guessed she was about twelve or thirteen. But though barely more than a child, such was her presence that he could only stand there and stare at her.

Earlier, Sven had told him that

Lolotea was related to the famous Mescalero warrior woman, Dahteste. Now, looking at her, Lawless saw she had inherited Dahteste's beauty and willowy grace. Bareheaded, with flawless persimmon-colored skin, she wore a beaded white doeskin dress and matching knee-high moccasins. Her sweet childlike face, pure as any saint, was framed by long, prematurely white, hair. Even more startling, her large almond-shaped eyes were completely covered by milky cataracts.

Surprised to find her so young, *and* blind, Lawless felt a strange spiritual aura permeating him like an invisible shroud. He could not describe the feeling. He just felt it, sensed it, was put at ease by it, and knew at once that he was in the presence of someone special; unearthly.

Lolotea motioned for him to place Joey before her.

Lawless obeyed, setting the unconscious boy on the white blanket. As he did he felt her hand, cool and gentle, lightly press against his forehead.

He looked at her, pleased and comforted by her touch.

Her lovely sightless face stared into his. Her expression was bright with the Great Spirit. It filled him with a peace he hadn't known since shooting Joey.

He did not see her lips move but heard her say, 'Leave now.'

Lawless obeyed. But as he reached the doorway, he could not resist looking back.

Lolotea now had one hand on Joey's forehead, the other over her heart. As if knowing Lawless was watching her, she looked at him and smiled. It was a simple smile, barely enough to tilt the corners of her mouth, yet its radiance lit up her entire face.

Lawless stood there, reluctant to leave.

Her milky, sightless eyes studied him. Again he did not see her lips move. Again he heard her voice, as musical as wind-chimes, telling him to return across the water and wait.

He left.

As he waded back across the creek, he sensed that a miracle was about to occur.

* * *

'What happened?' Violet said as Lawless entered the shaman's wickiup and sat opposite her and Sven. 'What did Lolotea say? Tell me, tell me.'

Lawless knew words could not properly describe what had happened. At the same time he did not want to disappoint Violet.

'She told me not to worry,' he lied.

Tears of relief filled Violet's eyes. 'I knew it,' she said excitedly. 'I just knew she'd be able to save Joey.'

Sven Bjorkman started to caution her. But he saw Lawless shake his head and fell silent.

'If I were you,' Lawless told Violet, 'I'd get some rest. I have a feeling this is going to take a while.'

'Yes,' she said as if trying to convince herself. 'I must rest. Joey's going to need me when he wakes up.' Leaning back against the wall of woven grasses, she tried to go to sleep.

Lawless swapped glances with Sven, neither man really believing that Joey would regain consciousness. Drawing his Colt, Lawless set it in his lap, pulled his hat down low and closed his eyes.

Outside, a warm breeze sprang up. It ruffled the surface of the creek and stirred the seashells over the door of the sacred wickiup. Their tinkling, mingled with Lolotea's faint rhythmic chanting, was the last sound Lawless heard before dozing off.

* * *

When he next awoke it was dark and someone was gently shaking him. Instantly he raised his Colt. It was only Sven. The Norwegian put a finger to his lips and pointed at Violet, asleep in the corner. Lawless rose soundlessly, holstered his .45 and followed Sven out of the wickiup.

Outside, Almighty Sky stood with Walking Man. Moonlight glinted on the blade of the ceremonial knife held by the old shaman. 'Your blood is needed, Tall Man.'

Lawless looked at Sven, who nodded. Trusting him, Lawless held out his hand.

Almighty Sky cut across the palm, drawing blood.

Walking Man caught the blood dripping from the wound in a white-painted clay bowl.

'What's this,' Lawless said, 'an eye for an eye?'

'Something close to that, yes,' Sven said.

When there was enough blood to cover the bottom of the bowl, Walking Man carried it across the creek to the sacred wickiup. Setting the bowl inside, he stepped back and took up his position beside Runs With Head Up.

'Now what?' Lawless said.

'*Ntse nt'ah*,' Almighty Sky said.

'Wait,' Sven translated.

Lawless went to the creek. Dipping his cut hand into the water, he knotted his kerchief around it and sat on one of the flat rocks the squaws had used to wash their clothes. Sven joined him. Lawless dug out the makings and handed them to Sven. The Norwegian built a cigarette and stuck it between Lawless's lips. Building another, he scratched a match on the rock and lit both their smokes.

They sat there smoking under a sickle moon, listening to a lonely coyote yip-yipping in the distance.

A shimmering reflection of the moon floated on the surface of the creek. Lawless gazed across it and contemplated the sacred wickiup. 'You ever seen her?'

'Once,' said Sven.

'I can see her face,' Lawless said, 'but I can't describe it.'

'I gave up trying,' Sven said. 'The irony is,' he added, 'we can see and can't describe her yet she's blind and can describe us.'

'How do you know that?'

'Almighty Sky told Raven. Said Lolotea asked about her one day. Called her *Ish-kay-nay* — which in Mescalero means 'boy who is indifferent to marriage', or in Raven's case a 'tomboy'. She was also the first to call my wife *Nah-tanh*, Apache for cornflower, which happens to be the color of her eyes.'

'Judas,' Lawless said.

'What makes it even stranger, Ingrid's never met her — ' He broke off as there was a noise on the opposite bank. Turning, they saw Walking Man wading across the creek toward them.

Almighty Sky met him at the water's edge. They spoke briefly. Then Walking Man returned across the creek.

Almighty Sky joined Lawless and Sven.

'It is ended,' he said. 'The boy's spirit has returned to our world. When the sun awakens, Runs With Head Up will bring him to you.'

12

Dawn came. The row of jagged bluffs to the east hid the rising sun, but they couldn't hide its magnificence. Gradually, lavender and rose streaks seeped out from behind the ridge flooding the heavens with color.

As if the approach of a new day was a signal, Runs With Head Up emerged from the sacred wickiup carrying Joey. The boy was conscious but very weak. His face was painted white and Lawless's blood encircled his eyes and lips, giving him a ghoulish effect. He gazed vacantly about him, trying to grasp where he was and why he was there. All he could see were Apaches — men, women and children from the village, lining the opposite bank. They blocked his view of everything behind them and he vaguely wondered where his sister was.

Runs With Head Up waded across the creek. He held Joey in his muscular arms as if the boy were weightless. When he reached the other bank the crowd stepped back, letting them pass through. The more curious Apaches touched Joey, hoping to attain spiritual enlightenment from this 'Child of the Pale Eyes' whom the Sacred One had resurrected.

Lawless watched everything from the wagon box. From his vantage point he could see Runs With Head Up approaching with Joey and behind them the crowd, chanting and shouting.

'Get ready,' he called out. 'Boy's on his way.'

Sven lowered the wagon tailgate and turned to face the oncoming Apaches. Kneeled in the wagon, Violet could contain herself no longer. Jumping up, she began waving excitedly to her brother.

'Joey! . . . Joe-eee!'

He raised his head, saw Violet waving to him from the wagon and feebly waved back.

Suddenly a golden eagle flew dangerously low over the village.

Its swooping shadow chased dogs to safety.

Mothers fearfully clutched their babies to their breasts.

The eagle, now a silhouette against the naked blue sky, winged ever upward and was soon lost in the sun. Its shrill screech echoed off the sandstone cliffs.

As if beckoned by the cry, Almighty Sky stepped from the council wickiup. Attired in his ceremonial dress he looked taller, prouder and more dignified than usual, while in his dark, lidded eyes burned the fires of his forefathers. Waiting until Runs With Head Up drew level with him, he fell in beside the young brave and together they walked to the wagon.

There, Almighty Voice turned to his people. They at once quieted. Raising his hands heavenward, he began speaking in Mescalero. He thanked the Great Spirit for allowing the

Sacred One to save the child of the Pale Eyes, adding that despite the many differences between the Apaches and their white brothers, he was happy to have lived long enough to see the day when their hatred for one another had diminished enough for the Pale Eyes to entrust the dying boy's life in the hands of the Sacred One.

He continued to speak for several more minutes. Then, when he was finished, he nodded to Runs With Head Up, who handed Joey over to Sven. Thanking Almighty Sky, and the Sacred One, Sven gently set the boy next to his sister in the wagon. Violet quickly wrapped a blanket around her brother and cuddled him against her. Tears of joy ran down her face as she began to comfort him.

It was time to leave.

The Apaches slowly dispersed and returned to their wickiups.

Lawless untied the reins from the wagon brake. As he waited for Sven to mount up, Lawless looked across the creek at the sacred white wickiup. Just before dawn he and Violet had wanted to thank Lolotea and tell her how grateful they were, but Almighty Sky had forbidden it. The Sacred One was with the Great Spirit, he said, and could not speak to anyone.

Disappointed, Violet asked Sven if he could change the old shaman's mind. The big Norwegian shook his head. In order to attain such an exalted level of holiness, Lolotea had to put herself in a deep trance that sometimes lasted for days. So she would not have been able to speak to them even if Almighty Sky had permitted it.

Now, as Lawless looked down from the wagon box, he saw Almighty Sky watching him from nearby. Lawless nodded respectfully, said, 'I ever ride this way again, Old One, I will bring you much coffee and tobacco.'

'Such kindness would make this old man happy,' Almighty Sky said. 'But you should know it is not meant to be.'

'Who told you that?'

'A blue owl came to me in the night and whispered we shall not stand before each other again.'

'This owl,' said Lawless, 'did he say why?'

Almighty Sky shook his head.

Having heard the shaman could predict the future, Lawless probed the Apache's dark eyes. He saw nothing in them to say Almighty Sky was lying yet he sensed the old man was hiding something, something that pertained to Lawless. Wondering what it was, and why the shaman wouldn't tell him, Lawless slapped the reins on the rumps of the horses.

The wagon rolled ahead. Behind him, Lawless heard Violet happily telling Joey that they were going home. He didn't hear her brother's weak reply but after all the boy had been through, Lawless could easily imagine how relieved Joey must be feeling.

The wagon hit a rut, jolting everyone.

As Lawless shifted, trying to find a more comfortable position on the box-seat, he tried to ignore the nagging premonition that kept warning him he was riding into trouble.

13

It was mid-morning when they arrived at the Morgans' spread. The sky had turned dark and thunderheads were gathering over the distant mountains. Ahead, the ranch house looked bleak and desolate on the horizon. As they got closer, lightning flashed over the hills to the west followed by the rumble of thunder.

Violet looked uneasily at the cattle and Clydesdales grazing on the scrubland. 'Will you stay and look after Joey,' she asked Lawless, 'while I try to track down the men? If our livestock gets spooked by the storm, they could blow wild and bust right on through the wire. Could take days to round them all up.'

'Be happy to,' Lawless said.

'I'll ride with you,' Sven told Violet. 'I don't have enough livestock to worry about stampeding.'

'What about your wife?' Lawless said, surprised that he even remembered Ingrid let alone felt concerned for her.

'She'll be fine. Storms don't bother her, or Raven for that matter. Like everything else in life they pretty much adapt and ride things out.' He chuckled ruefully. 'I swear, if anything happened to me, the two of them would not only survive, they'd lick the ranch into better shape than it is right now.'

'Maybe so. But the desert's no place for a woman and child to be alone. Especially close to the border like you folks are. Never know when *bandidos* or renegades might cross over and . . .' Lawless left the rest unsaid.

'Ingrid and I have discussed that,' Sven said. 'Took some fancy talking on my part, but she finally agreed that if things got too tough she'd pack up and take Raven to her stepbrother, Reece, a well-to-do banker who lives in California.'

Lawless said no more. But, as they

rode across the flatland and picked up the trail leading to the ranch house, he chided himself for the thoughts he was feeling for another man's wife.

* * *

It was sprinkling when Lawless stopped the wagon in front of the ranch house. The thunder and lightning were now much closer, the threat of a bad storm imminent.

'You take Joey inside,' Lawless said to Sven, 'while I unhitch the team.'

The big easy-going Norwegian nodded, seemingly content to be told what to do, and swung down from his horse.

'I'll go saddle up,' Violet said, jumping off the wagon. 'We shouldn't have to ride too far to find Miguel and Rios. Most likely, seeing the storm coming, they're already heading home. Joey,' she added, 'you're to do exactly as Mr Lawless tells you, you hear?' She ran off before he could argue.

The jolting ride had not been easy on

Joey. He hadn't complained about the pain, but it had taken most of the fire out of him and he offered no resistance as Sven climbed into the wagon and gently helped him up.

Meanwhile, Lawless unhitched the traces and led the two wet horses toward the barn. Ahead, Violet opened the big double doors and hurried inside.

Thunder boomed overhead. It startled the team and, placid as they were, the horses reared up almost tearing the reins from Lawless' hands. 'Whoa, whoa . . . ' He fought to pull them down. 'Easy now . . . easy . . . ' It took a few seconds but finally the horses calmed and let Lawless lead them to the barn.

As he reached the big double doors a muffled scream came from inside. Dropping the reins Lawless ran into the barn.

Two men faced him, both wearing deputy stars, both holding cocked carbines.

A third man straddled Violet, pinning

her to the ground with his knees. His hand was clamped over her mouth. Above it her gray-green eyes were wide with fear.

Lawless tensed, hand poised above his gun, ready to kill all three.

'Don't try it,' one man warned. 'We ain't aiming to harm you or the girl, not unless you go for your iron.'

Tempted, Lawless decided he might not be able to gun them all down before one managed to kill, and not willing to risk her life he dropped his hand to his side. Hunkering down in front of her, he asked her if she was all right.

She nodded.

Lawless rose and faced the other two men. 'Let her up, or I'll make you use those shooters.'

They sensed he wasn't bluffing. The man who'd spoken first, Cory Rivers, nodded to the man astride Violet. The man let Violet up but kept her covered with his six-gun.

'Unbuckle your belt,' Rivers told Lawless. 'Kick it over here.'

Lawless obeyed without argument.
'Outside,' Rivers said.
Again, Lawless obeyed him. The three men, with Violet ahead of them, followed him out of the barn.
It was raining hard now. It came slashing down, driven sideways by gusts of wind, turning the ground into mud. Lawless splashed through the puddles, squinting against the slanting rain. Ahead, he saw three more men, armed with shotguns, standing outside the door of the log-house.
Was this the trouble his premonition had warned him about?

* * *

Inside the house Sheriff Tishman sat drinking coffee at the table. He was dry, indicating he'd been there a while, and looked relaxed except for the tension in his eyes. His regular deputy, Lonnie Davis, a skinny man with a few greasy hairs combed over his scalp and a bulging Adam's apple, stood behind him holding a scattergun.

The lamp on the table was unlit. Due to the storm very little light came through the curtained window and the room was dim at best. A shadowy figure guarding the door to the rear bedrooms was barely visible.

The front door opened with a wind-blown rush. Lawless and Violet swept in, drenched to the skin, followed by Rivers. All three were chased by a gust of wind that spattered everyone with rain. China rattled on the shelves and the curtains flapped — then Rivers kicked the door shut and everything was silent and still.

'Well, now,' the sheriff said to Lawless, 'I see you decided to give Miss Morgan my regards after all.' Jerking his thumb toward the bedrooms, he added to Violet, 'Too bad you shot the wrong fella.'

'I wish it had been you,' she hissed.

The sheriff clucked his tongue. 'Shame on you, missy. Don't you know it's against the law to threaten a peace officer? Why, I'd be in my rights if I laid you 'cross my knee and spanked the daylights out of you.'

'Just you try,' Violet said, 'and when my men get back they'll — '

'Men? Mean them two greasers you got riding for you?' The sheriff leaned back and laughed. 'Hell, you can forget about them, missy. After the boys dragged 'em around behind their horses for a spell, they was only too eager to hightail it back to chili-land.'

'You bastard!' Violet lunged for the sheriff, but Lawless pulled her back.

'If you're all done baiting her,' he said, 'maybe you'd like to tell us why you're here?'

The sheriff pulled a document from his vest pocket and told his deputy to light the lamp. Lonnie Davis obeyed. Removing the glass shield, he struck a match on his jeans and held it to the wick. Light flooded the room. It not only illuminated the document in the sheriff's hands, but revealed the man standing by the bedroom door.

He was a small man, slim and handsome with sandy hair, large blue eyes with thick lashes any woman would envy and a winning smile. Because of his diminutive size and boyish good looks, it was hard to judge his age or his profession. His tailored gray suit, string tie, and expensive hand-tooled boots didn't help either — they suggested he might be a rich businessman, successful rancher, or possibly even a riverboat gambler. But he was none of those things. And as he stepped forward, closer to the light, the tools of his trade could be seen on his hips: two ivory-handled, nickel-plated Colt .44s that poked from well-oiled, tied-down holsters.

Recognizing him, Lawless hid his surprise and grimly eyed Sheriff Tishman. 'Didn't take you long to hire my replacement.'

The sheriff chuckled. 'Hear that, Latigo — Mr Lawless, here, thinks you're working for me.'

'He knows me better than that,'

Latigo Rawlins said.

'I know you don't sell your gun just for wages,' Lawless said.

'Or work for a sheriff who coils when he sits,' Latigo added.

Sheriff Tishman reddened, swallowed hard, but kept his composure. Handing the document to Violet, he said: 'As of right now, you and your brother no longer own this spread.'

'The bank can't do that!'

'Read it and see, missy. It's all written down, neat and legal.'

'I don't believe you!' She turned to Lawless. 'Bria — Mr Edfors would never kick Joey and me off the ranch. He told me so himself, a hundred times.'

Lawless took the document from her, scanned it. 'Seems he changed his mind. Like the sheriff says, it's legal.'

'B-but he promised! Gave me his word that we'd never have to worry. Why, he even asked me to mar — '

'What?' said Lawless as she broke off. 'What did he ask you?'

Violet blushed, too embarrassed to explain.

Sheriff Tishman grinned, enjoying this. 'Reckon you played him for a love-sick fool once too often, missy. Worm's finally turned. And if you'll excuse me for gloating, it's about time. Now' — he took out a big Hamilton timepiece and checked the time — 'you got exactly one hour to gather up your personal belongings, load 'em on your wagon — which by the way Mr Edfors kindly says you can keep — and ride on out of here.'

'Don't be a fool,' Lawless said. 'You've seen Joey's condition. He can't leave here, not for a week or two at least.'

The sheriff rose to his full height, dug out a bag of lemon drops and put one in his mouth. 'I don't know what your play in this is, *amigo*, but unless you're anxious to be behind bars, best get on your horse and keep riding till you reach Arizona. Oh, and by the way. Don't count on saving my life to mean anything. You already traded that favor to keep Joey out of jail.'

Behind him, Deputy Lonnie Davis cocked the hammers on his shotgun and aimed it at Lawless.

Unfazed, Lawless turned to Latigo Rawlins. 'What about you?'

'What about me?'

'I've known you to do some mighty ugly things, Lefty, but evicting a girl and a shot-up boy in a rainstorm — surely you haven't stooped that low?'

Latigo grinned. 'If you're trying to shame me into backing you, Ben, forget it. My conscience died on me in the cradle.'

'Ben?' the sheriff said, disappointed. 'That's his real name?'

'Yep.'

'Not Will?'

'Uh-uh. Will's his cousin.'

'You know that for true?'

'Sure. I know Will Lawless. He, Ben and I used to — '

'That's enough,' Lawless warned.

The little gunfighter bristled. 'You

giving me orders now?'

Before Lawless could answer, the sheriff said, 'If they look that much alike, how can you be sure which one it was?'

'Easy. Tell Ben, here, to unbutton his shirt.'

'Do it,' the sheriff ordered.

Lawless didn't move. 'You're making a mistake,' he told Latigo.

'How you figure that?'

'You're counting on being faster than me.'

'I am faster than you,' Latigo said. 'I'm faster than anybody.' He spoke casually, without bravado, his voice surprisingly deep for someone his size. 'But that ain't what I'm counting on. I'm figuring you don't want that thundergun the deputy's holding to go off. 'Cause at this range, it won't only blow daylight through you but through that little gal next to you, too.'

Lawless sighed. He knew when to fold. Grudgingly he unbuttoned his shirt, revealing the ugly white scar circling his neck.

Sickened, Violet quickly looked away.

Both deputies did the same.

Sheriff Tishman whistled softly. 'Godawmighty,' he said. His hand strayed to the rope burns around his own neck. 'How come you ain't dead?'

'I wonder about that myself sometimes,' Lawless said.

Latigo chuckled. 'The *rurales* would rest easier if you were.'

'They the ones who hanged you?' the sheriff said.

Lawless made a sound that could have meant anything and buttoned up his shirt.

But the damage had been done. Even though the scar was no longer visible, the others could still visualize it along with the horrors it conjured up, and remained silent.

The only sound was the rain hammering on the roof and against the window.

Lawless said, 'How about it, Sheriff? Will you let Violet and her brother rest up here till morning? A night's sleep might mean all the difference to Joey.'

'Couldn't even if I wanted to.'

'Why not?'

'I'm here to uphold the law. And the law wants 'em off this property — now.'

'Law be damned,' Violet said contemptuously. 'Brian Edfors is the one making you do this. It's his way of spiting me for refusing to marry him.'

'What's been going on 'tween you and Mr Edfors is no concern of mine,' the sheriff said. 'Judge Ainsley signed this eviction notice, and he's the one who told me to carry out the instructions. I aim to do just that.' Turning to Deputy Davis, he added, 'Bring Bjorkman and the boy out.'

14

The storm had moved on by the time Lawless and Sven finished loading the wagon with trunks and boxes holding Violet and Joey's personal belongings. The sky was still overcast, but the dark clouds were breaking up and the rain had slackened to a depressing drizzle. Only the ground remained a reminder of the recent deluge: it was now a quagmire in which boots sank up to the ankles.

Earlier, Sven had insisted the Morgans stay at his place while Joey recuperated. Violet, too proud to accept charity, agreed on one condition: that she would be allowed to earn their keep by doing chores. Sven grudgingly agreed, but warned Violet not to let his daughter talk her into doing her chores, too. Raven hated doing chores more than anything, he said, and when she put her mind to it, could charm the crows out of the trees.

Now, with brother and sister snugly tucked under a slicker in the back of the wagon, Sven and Lawless finished hitching up the team and prepared to leave.

Flanked by his deputies, Sheriff Tishman watched from the doorway of the house. He was the only one who was happy about what was going on. He rocked gently on his heels, thumbs tucked in his belt, enjoying the pain he was causing Violet and Joey.

'Go ahead, smirk,' she said bitterly. 'You haven't seen the last of us. Just 'cause you forced Joey and me to leave doesn't mean we won't be back.'

'Sh-she's right,' Joey said weakly. 'And next time I jump you on the trail, you big tub of fat, won't be nobody to save you from a rope.'

Lawless sensed the boy had gone too far. About to climb on to the wagon, he saw the sheriff angrily spin around and storm into the house.

There, he grabbed the hurricane lamp and hurled it against the wall. The glass shield shattered, kerosene splashing everywhere. Flames flared up, quickly engulfing the curtains and log walls beside the window. Picking up a second, unlighted lamp the sheriff threw it against the opposite wall and ran out. The flames spread to the spilled kerosene, ignited, and within moments the house was ablaze. Smoke from the wet logs spewed everywhere.

With a cry of dismay, Violet pushed the slicker aside and scrambled over the side of the wagon. Sven whirled his horse around and grabbed her before she reached the ground. She screamed for him to let her go. When he wouldn't, she tried to break free. But Sven was too strong and finally Violet stopped struggling and burst into tears. Sven held her to him and did his best to calm her.

He'd almost succeeded when Sheriff Tishman approached with his deputies.

He grinned mockingly at Violet and Joey.

'Reckon next time, you young'uns won't be so damn' quick to spout off.'

Incensed, Violet again tried to break loose. But she was helpless in Sven's powerful grip. Finally she stopped struggling and cursed the sheriff through her tears. Joey joined in. But their rage and frustration only amused the big lawman and he stood there, contentedly sucking on a lemon drop.

It was then Lawless came out of the swirling smoke.

He didn't walk out. He seemed to appear, like a shadow in sunlight, the crackling roar of the flames hiding any sound he made as he walked toward the sheriff. Though none of the fury he felt showed on his face, and he carried no weapon, there was a vengeful lethalness about him that was frightening.

Instantly, the deputies covered him with their rifles.

Lawless kept walking.

Sheriff Tishman wet his lips uneasily.

'I ain't never shot an unarmed man, mister. But if you'n that wagonload of whelps don't haul out of here, I swear I'll make you the first.'

Lawless showed no sign of hearing him.

If there was any fear, it was in the hearts of the armed deputies.

'Ben . . . ' Sven rode up alongside him. 'He means it.'

Lawless stopped, less than a foot from the deputies' rifles, and pinned the sheriff with an unforgiving stare.

'Ben!'

Lawless came back from a lonely, dark, far-off place.

A tree . . . a hangman's noose . . . a ring of riders, mocking him as he slowly choked . . . the images gradually faded from his mind. When they were gone, so was the rage blazing in his soul and his amber eyes looked at Sven as if seeing him for the first time.

'Time to go,' Sven said gently.

Lawless nodded and, without looking at the sheriff or the deputies, he turned and climbed on to the wagon.

'Hold up, Ben . . .' Latigo approached from the barn. 'Might need this.' Standing on tiptoe, he handed Lawless his gunbelt.

Lawless nodded his thanks, snapped the reins and the wagon rolled away.

15

They hadn't traveled more than fifty yards when a shot rang out . . . followed by a sharp cry of pain. Lawless reined up and they all looked back.

Sheriff Tishman lay writhing in the mud near the burning house.

Standing over him, gun in hand, was Latigo Rawlins. The little gunfighter callously watched as the sheriff continued to squirm and clutch at his bleeding foot. His agonized yelps carried on the wind. Latigo leaned closer and for a moment it looked like he might shoot the lawman again. Then, ever unpredictable, he holstered his six-gun, wiped the mud from his boots on the sheriff's jeans, and carefully picked his way between the puddles to the barn.

The deputies, gathered in a half-circle around the sheriff, did nothing to stop him. They were only too glad to see him go. A few helped the sheriff to his feet. Others hurried behind the barn where their horses were tied.

After a little, Latigo Rawlins trotted out of the barn astride a rangy golden sorrel that had been bred for both speed and stamina. With a mocking wave to the sheriff, he rode off.

'What the devil . . . ?' began Sven.

'Wonder what happened?' Violet said.

Lawless shrugged. 'Most likely, Tishman gave Lefty hell for giving me my gun.'

'He shot him in the foot just for hollering at him?'

'That's Latigo. He doesn't take to being hollered at.'

'But Tishman's the sheriff,' Joey said. 'The law.'

Lawless grinned, despite himself. 'That didn't stop you from stringing him up, did it now?' He watched Rawlins growing smaller on the horizon. 'Wouldn't stop Lefty, either. I've seen him kill men, including lawmen, for a lot less.' He clucked the team into action and the wagon rolled ahead.

Sven rode alongside Lawless, saying: 'You seem to know this Latigo Rawlins pretty well.'

'We've ridden some.'

'That surprises me.'

Lawless made no comment.

'From the way you talk, you've obviously had schooling . . . maybe came from a fine educated family. Latigo, on the other hand, is no different than any other gunmen I've run across — 'cept maybe for his fancy duds.'

'He's different, believe me,' Lawless said.

'How?'

'He's never felt remorse.'

Sven waited for Lawless to explain further. When he didn't, Sven said, 'Any idea who he works for?'

'Uh-uh.'

'If you had to guess.'

Lawless shrugged. 'Who's the most important man in the territory?'

'That's easy. Stillman J. Stadtlander.'

'The cattleman?'

Sven ruefully shook his head. 'You've been drifting too long, Ben. Mr Stadtlander is much more than a cattleman now. He's the power behind the throne, as we say in Norway. With his money and influence, he either controls or has a finger in just about everything from here to Las Cruces and east to El Paso — cattle, land, mining, the works. I've never had dealings with him, but those who have say he's greedy and ruthless and has lawmen, judges — even politicians — all eating out of his hand.'

'They don't have any choice,' Violet said, 'not according to Brian Edfors.' Sniffing back her tears, she stared sadly at the burning house she and Joey had once called home. Most of it was consumed by flames now and smoke spiraled up to the clouds. 'Folks are too afraid of what he or his son, Slade, might do if they went up against him.'

'That's your answer then,' Lawless

said. ' 'Long as I've known him, Lefty's only worked for the lead steer. And sometimes even that riles him. Then he goes back to being a bounty hunter and swears never to take orders from anyone again.' He frowned, puzzled, before adding, 'When you chew on it, it doesn't make sense. His being here, I mean. Edfors may be able to buffalo folks in Borega Springs, but that doesn't make him important enough to interest a high-stakes killer like Latigo Rawlins.'

'Or a man like Stillman J. Stadtlander,' Sven said.

'Well, someone must have sent him,' Violet said, 'or he wouldn't have been here.'

Lawless knew she was right. But he had no answer.

They rode on across the humid, muddy scrubland in silence.

A road runner flashed in front of them, startling the sleepy horses. They pricked their ears and snorted, saliva spraying everywhere. Then as the fast-moving bird vanished into a gully, they wearily plodded on.

'He came to our house once,' Joey said, raising up on his elbows.

'Who did, son?'

'Mr Stadtlander. Remember?' he said to Violet. 'He rode a big mean black horse — a Morgan, I think he called it. It was right pretty to look at but it kept trying to bite and kick everyone.'

'That's right,' Violet said. 'Now I remember. It was back when Pa was alive and Aunt Sara was visiting.'

'What did he want?' Lawless said.

'Pa never said. But whatever it was, Pa wouldn't agree and that made Mr Stadtlander awful angry. Told Pa that he'd be sorry. Said what he couldn't get with honey, he'd get with vinegar.'

'Sounds like Mr Stadtlander, all right,' Sven said.

'Was Latigo with him?' Lawless asked.

'I don't think so. Was he, Joey?'

'No. But there was a man just like him.'

'A gunfighter, you mean?'

'Uh-huh.'

'Remember what he looked like?'

'Tall, like you. Only his hair was blacker and he had these scary pale blue eyes that seemed to shoot right through you.'

The description fitted several gunmen Lawless had met over the years, but all of them were territorial and he doubted if any of them had left their home states and settled in New Mexico. 'Remember his name, do you?'

Joey shook his head. 'But it was a funny name. You know, different. I remember 'cause after Mr Stadtlander and his men left I asked Pa about it. Asked him if he'd ever heard a name like that before and he said he hadn't. But he knew who the man was. Said he was a shootist, maybe the best ever.'

They rode on, Lawless doing all he could to keep the wagon from bumping around.

* * *

Now in the distance they could see the wind-pump, buildings and corrals of the Bjorkman ranch. South of the ranch was the border and to the north-east a misty row of far-off peaks made up the horizon. One or two had snow on them and Lawless guessed he was looking at the Cookes Range.

'I'll ride ahead,' Sven said, 'let Ingrid know we're coming.' He kicked his horse into an easy gallop and rode off.

Lawless watched him riding away. He told himself that he could only stay one night at the Bjorkman's. Being around Sven's wife any longer than that, he knew, might stir up feelings that long ago he'd buried deep within him as a protection against ever loving any woman — only to lose her when circumstances he couldn't control forced him to ride on.

Just then it hit him.

'Moonlight!' he said. 'Gabriel Moonlight. Was that his name, Joey?'

Joey didn't answer.

Lawless looked over his shoulder and

saw that the boy had fallen asleep with his head on his sister's shoulder. Violet, worn out by crying, was also sleeping.

Deciding not to wake them, Lawless faced front again and flicked the reins, guiding the horses around a large muddy pothole in the trail.

As he sat there on the box-seat, hearing but not listening to the wagon creaking, traces jingling, hoofs plopping, he wondered if he was right. Could Gabriel Moonlight really be the gunman Joey had seen with Stadtlander? Could fate, after so many years, have actually brought the three of them together again?

And if so, for what purpose?

Killing each other?

Lawless frowned, troubled by the idea, and thought grimly, Gabe, Lefty and me, all within fifty miles of each other. Jesus Joseph Mary, what were the chances of that ever happening?

BOOK TWO

16

When Ingrid greeted them at the door of the log-house Lawless realized she was even prettier than he remembered. From the wagon box, where he sat holding the reins, he watched as she kissed her husband on the cheek, her lovely face momentarily buried in his beard, and then hugged Violet and told her and Joey how welcome they were and how sorry she was that Mr Edfors had seen fit to evict them while they were still mourning the loss of their father. For now she added, Violet would be sharing Raven's bedroom, while Joey would sleep on a cot in a corner near the stove. Later, when the army put a stop to the raiding and Sven went back to work, hopefully he could afford to buy enough lumber to build them their own cabin.

'You'd do that for us?' Violet said to

Ingrid and Sven.

'Why not?' Sven said. 'We're neighbors, aren't we?'

'Y-yes, but — '

'If situations were reversed, your pa would've done the same for us.'

Violet nodded, but she wasn't so sure. Her father had often told her that Sven was the most generous and giving man he'd ever met; far more generous and giving than he was. 'We'll pay you back,' she promised. 'I don't know how but we will, won't we, Joey?'

He nodded and, trying to sound manly, said, 'Got my word on it, Mr Bjorkman.'

'Thanks, but it isn't necessary,' Sven said. 'Ingrid and I are just happy we can share our lives with you.'

'I'll also help with the chores,' Violet said to Ingrid. 'So will Joey when he's better. Won't you, Joey?'

'Yes'm,' he said wearily.

'That'll be wonderful,' Ingrid said. 'Because it seems my other helper manages to conveniently disappear whenever she's needed.' She looked meaningfully at her husband as she spoke and he smiled uneasily and glanced about him.

'Where is Raven anyway?'

'Where she always is,' Ingrid said crossly. 'Out there somewhere.' She gestured toward the desert, adding, 'You really must talk to her. I swear to goodness, the child pays absolutely no attention to me.'

'Now, now,' Sven said soothingly. 'It's only temporary. She's just going through a stage. It's hard on her too. She has no one her own age to play with, and that's forced her to make friends with the Apaches and critters in the desert.'

'I don't mind her befriending wild animals,' Ingrid said, 'or learning about the desert from the Mescaleros. In fact it's good, because then I don't have to worry about her when she disappears for hours on end. But what I do mind is when she neglects her chores and acts as if she herself is feral and not obligated to mind me or what I say.'

Sven sighed, torn between keeping his wife happy and corralling his beloved daughter. 'I understand. And you're absolutely right. But Raven has never been like ordinary children, we both know that. And I doubt if she'll ever change, no matter what we tell her, or however many spankings I give her.'

'So that supposedly excuses her behavior?'

''Course not. And Raven has to realize that or take her licks. But meanwhile, try to be patient with her. Give her time. Eventually she'll come around. I know she will.'

'But you'll talk to her just the same?'

'Promise.'

'I'm going to hold you to that, Mr Bjorkman, don't think I'm not.' Ingrid looked at Lawless, eyes blue as cornflowers, and said, 'I hope you don't mind, but the barn's all I have to offer you.'

'Barn's fine,' he said.

'Good. I'll have Raven bring you

some blankets. And of course you'll eat with us.'

'Thank you, ma'am.' He held her gaze, feeling captured as he did and for a moment thought he saw a faint blush creeping into her cheeks. Then it was gone, so quickly he knew he must have imagined it. Turning to Sven, he said: 'I'll unhitch the team while you get everyone settled.'

Sven nodded. 'After supper, Ben, I'll ask you to help me unload the wagon. There's room at the back of the barn to store everything. And then tomorrow, you'n me will clear a space for you up in the loft. Can't have you sleeping down with the horses.'

'I don't mind,' Lawless said.

'I do,' Sven said. 'By golly, it's been a long dry spell since we've had any guests around here. And I'll be truthful with you, Ben, since the 'Paches put on paint and the surveyor work dried up, I've missed not having other men to talk to, maybe play poker with, or down a beer or two — '

'Sweetheart,' Ingrid interrupted gently, 'I think Mr Lawless knows what you mean.'

'Yes, yes, 'course he does.' Sven grinned sheepishly, a boy in a man's body. 'Don't mind me, Ben. Like Ingrid says: I tend to get overly enthusiastic at times and then I ramble on and on.' Before Lawless could say anything, the big Norwegian grabbed one of Violet and Joey's trunks from the wagon and carried it effortlessly indoors.

Ingrid smiled shyly at Lawless. 'It's been hard on him,' she said. 'He loved his work and feels lost without it — '

'No need to apologize, ma'am. Your husband's a fine man. Maybe the finest I've met.'

'I know that, Mr Lawless. And I wasn't apologizing. I just wanted you to understand why he's so pleased you're here.' Turning, she slipped her arm around Joey's waist, 'C'mon, let's get you inside.' Violet did the same and together they helped him into the house.

Lawless clucked the horses into action and drove the heavily loaded wagon to the barn. It was only a short distance but several times the wheels became stuck in the mud. But each time at his urging the team managed to pull them free and finally Lawless reined up outside the barn.

Jumping down he unhitched the traces and led the big mud-spattered horses inside. There, as he was about to remove the harnesses, he glimpsed something move in the hayloft above him. He dived behind the horses, Colt leaping into his hand, and rolled into the nearest stall. He lay motionless on the hay, heart thudding, waiting for whatever it was to move again. The memory of shooting Joey was vivid in his mind and he warned himself to make sure he saw his target clearly before he pulled the trigger.

When nothing stirred, he inched forward on his belly and elbows and peered around the wooden divider.

Instantly a small round stone smacked

against the wood dangerously close to his head.

Lawless flinched and ducked back behind the divider.

He heard a faint giggle. 'No need to be scared,' a girl's voice said above him. 'If I'd wanted to hit you, I would've.'

Lawless relaxed, lowered the hammer on his Colt and got to his feet. 'Show yourself, girl. C'mon,' he added when no one appeared. 'No more games.'

Raven stepped from behind a roof support, holding a homemade slingshot and chewing on piece of straw. Resting one bare foot on the top rung of the loft-ladder, she stared at him insolently.

Lawless holstered his six-gun and nudged his hat back on his head. 'Your folks think you're out in the desert.'

'I was. Now I'm here.'

'Don't be impertinent.'

'What's that mean?'

'Cheeky — disrespectful.'

'That weren't my intention. I was just answering you, not sassing you.' She continued to stare at him, head cocked sideways like an inquisitive crow, her short hair just as black and shiny, as if trying to make up her mind about him.

'When you're all done staring,' he said, 'come on down.'

'Wasn't staring. Was wondering . . . '

'About what?'

'Why you shot Joey.'

He frowned, wondering how she knew.

'Don't look so surprised, mister. Anything goes on at the reservation, I mostly hear about it.'

'Then you already have your answer, so why ask me to repeat it?'

Raven was stumped for an answer. Tucking the slingshot into her jeans, she climbed down the ladder until she got halfway then pretended to lose her footing, gave a cry and fell backward. Lawless lunged to grab her. But it was all an act. Twisting in midair, she landed catlike on her feet on a pile of hay.

'See,' she said. 'I can move fast too.'

He felt like spanking her. But he said

only: 'Let's see how fast you can help me with these horses.'

* * *

That night it was crowded around the table. Supper was just stew and bread, with Ingrid apologizing for not having a pie or even wild berries for dessert. 'If only you'd only told me earlier you were coming,' she lamented. 'I — ' She broke off, realizing how insensitive her remark was, and then pressed her hand fondly over Violet's. 'I'm so sorry, dear. Forgive me. I wasn't thinking . . . '

'It's all right, Mrs Bjorkman.' Violet fought back her tears. 'I know you didn't mean anything by it. Besides, this is a wonderful meal. Far better than what I used to cook for Joey or the men. Right, Joey?'

Her brother nodded and continued mopping up his gravy with a hunk of bread. He could only use his right hand. The left arm was now held in a sling made from one of Sven's old work shirts and any abrupt movement made him wince with pain.

'Why do you think I married her?' Sven said, trying to lighten the mood. 'There were plenty of other women to choose from in the village. But none of them could bake bread or charm a pie out of the oven like my Ingrid.'

'Why, Sven Bjorkman! And here all along I thought it was because of my dowry.'

'Dowry!' Sven thumped the table with his beefy hand so hard it rattled the dishes. 'If it was money or possessions I was after, woman, I would've stayed in Norway and married the widow Johanssen. Her dowry came with a castle.'

'Sweetheart, I was only teasing — '

'No, no,' he said, as if she hadn't spoken, 'dowries had nothing to do with why I asked you to be my wife, begged you in fact, and I think you know that . . . have known it all along.'

Ingrid smiled, faintly embarrassed, and raising his hand to her lips kissed his fingers, one at a time. 'You're a dear sweet man, my husband,' she said softly.

Watching them from across the table, Lawless realized for the first time in his life he envied another man. It was a feeling he didn't like and thanking Ingrid for the meal he excused himself, saying it was time he bedded down.

'So early?' Sven said. 'I was hoping we could play some two-handed whiskey poker before turning in.'

'Another time,' Lawless said. He went out.

'Did I say something to offend him?' Sven asked his wife. 'If I did I surely didn't mean to.'

'No,' she assured him. 'He's just tired, like all of us.'

'That ain't it,' Raven said sullenly. It was the first time she'd spoken since they all sat down to eat and everyone looked at her. 'He just wanted to be alone.'

'How do you know that?' said her father. 'Did he say something to you about it?'

'Didn't have to. I just know.'

'Oh, Raven, for goodness sake stop trying to be mysterious,' her mother said. 'You've only just met Mr Lawless, same as the rest of us. There's no possible way you know what he's thinking.'

'That's what you think,' Raven said. 'But you're wrong. I talked to him in the barn while we were taking care of the horses. I knew it then and I know it now. I can tell. He's just like me, wants to be alone. So there.'

'Raven!' her father said sternly. 'Don't talk to your mother like that. Now apologize. You hear?'

Raven looked at her father, then her mother, her huge black eyes blazing with resentment. 'I'll apologize,' she said, 'but I won't mean it. And you can't make me.' She turned to her mother, 'I'm sorry,' and pushing back from the table, ran into her bedroom.

Sven stared after her as if unable to believe what had just happened. He then asked Violet and Joey to excuse

Raven's bad manners, adding that something must have upset her. She wasn't usually like that. 'I'll go talk to her,' he added to Ingrid.

'Leave her be,' she said. 'Tomorrow's soon enough.' Rising, she began collecting the dirty dishes. Violet immediately jumped up and helped her. Joey looked across the table at Sven. 'When I'm better, Mr Bjorkman, I'll play cards with you. Or even checkers. Pa taught me how before he . . . he was killed.'

Sven smiled and affectionately tousled Joey's hair. 'I'll look forward to that, son.'

'Me, too,' said Joey. Then, as Sven got his pipe and tobacco from a cupboard beside the pantry and returned to the table, he added, 'Pa used to smoke a pipe just like that, Mr Bjorkman. Same kind of tobacco, too.'

'I know,' Sven said. 'He's the one who got me started using it.'

'Thank goodness he did,' put in Ingrid. 'I never liked that other blend you used. Smelled like old socks burning.'

Sven rolled his eyes, gave Joey a 'we-men-must-stick-together' wink, and began patiently packing his pipe.

Joey beamed. It was one of the few times he had smiled since losing his father and Violet, watching her brother as she stacked the dirty dishes, felt a sense of relief. Maybe some good would come out of losing their home after all.

17

The next morning, before the first rooster crowed, Lawless stood with his arms resting on a corral fence watching the sky lightening above the hills in the east. It was cold, desert-cold, and a wind blowing up from Mexico tugged at his hair and chilled the back of his neck. Unable to chase Ingrid from his mind, he'd slept little during the night and his eyes felt raw and gritty. Finishing his third cigarette since rising, he flipped it into the empty corral and for the umpteenth time promised himself that right after breakfast he would ask Sven to take him into nearby Santa Rosa. There, hopefully he could find some kind of temporary work until he had enough money to buy a horse and saddle, and then head for Arizona.

Footsteps behind him interrupted his

thoughts. He turned and saw Ingrid, a basket of eggs on her arm, leaving the barn. She waved to him, took a few more steps toward the house then stopped, turned, and came up to him.

'Good morning.'

''Morning, ma'am.'

'I hope you got some sleep. Sven's been meaning to fix those loose boards that bang around when the wind blows, but — '

'I slept just fine, thanks,' Lawless said. He noticed she'd left her long tawny hair hanging loose and he couldn't help thinking how fresh and pretty she looked with the wind blowing through it.

His steady gaze made her self-conscious. She brushed some loose strands back from her face, saying, 'I must look an awful mess. But Sven likes it when I let my hair down at night and . . . ' Her voice trailed off.

There was an awkward silence. It wasn't that they didn't know what to say, just how to say it.

'He's a lucky man,' Lawless said quietly.

'No, I'm a lucky woman,' Ingrid said. 'What Sven said at supper was true: there *were* plenty of other women available in our village. All of them eager to marry him.'

'Not you, though.'

'What do you mean?'

'He said he begged you to marry him.'

'Oh . . . that.' She blushed, as if caught in a lie, said quickly, 'Sven was just joking. Believe me, he was a truly fine catch.'

'That why you married him?'

'I married him,' she said firmly, 'because I loved him, Mr Lawless.'

'Ahh.'

'You don't believe me?'

'Why would you lie?'

'I wouldn't.' She looked away and shifted uneasily on her feet.

Lawless waited for her to continue. But she didn't and there was another awkward silence.

'Well,' she said finally, 'I must go make breakfast. Sven's one of those men who can't start the day without a good meal inside him. I swear,' she added, 'you could tell him Geronimo was on the warpath again and he'd say, 'Please, Ingrid, not before I've eaten'.'

Lawless smiled. 'I feel the same way about coffee, ma'am.'

'In that case, I'll be sure to have a cup waiting for you.' She turned away, took a few hesitant steps and then looked back at him. 'You're leaving us today, aren't you?'

His tight-lipped silence confirmed she was right.

She hesitated, teeth torturing her lower lip, then said: 'I know it's none of my business, Mr Lawless, but may I ask what your reason is for going so soon?'

'Got things to do.'

'Things?'

He nodded.

'In Arizona?'

'Yes. How'd you know?'

'Sven told me. Last night before we

went to sleep. Said if Joey hadn't shot your horse, you'd be in Arizona by now.'

'I meant, about my leaving?'

'Oh-h . . . I . . . It was something my daughter said.'

'Raven?'

'Yes. She's only a child but she's very astute that way. I don't know why, certainly neither Sven nor I are intuitive . . . but Raven, well, she's always been able to sense how people are feeling . . . '

Lawless didn't doubt that.

'I wish you wouldn't,' Ingrid said.

He frowned, surprised. 'You asking me to stay?'

'Y-yes . . . Not for me, you understand — for my husband.'

'Go on.'

'Last night was the happiest I've seen him in weeks, months even.'

'What's that got to do with me?'

'Well, it's hard to explain, but . . . '

'On account of his penchant for male company?'

'Penchant?'

'His love of.'

'Oh. Yes . . . you could put it that way.' She studied him for a moment, wondering who he really was and where he was from, then lowered her eyes and ran her fingers gently over the eggs.

'I wouldn't worry about that anymore, ma'am. He has the boy now. He'll be fine.'

'I hope so. It's just . . . '

'What?'

'He so admires you, enjoys being with you, having you around to talk to and . . . I mean . . . you see it's a man's company he needs, not a boy's. It seems to fire him up. Last night he was talking how he wants you to help him fix things up around here. Of course he'll pay you. It won't be much but — Do you really have to leave today?' she pressed. 'I mean couldn't you stay a little longer — just a few days even?'

He looked into her upturned face, her pleading blue eyes, and saw nothing but trouble ahead. But despite the warning, he heard himself say: 'A few days?'

She nodded, willing to accept any offer that would keep him there.

He shrugged. 'Reckon I can do that.'

'Oh, that's wonderful. Thank you, Mr Lawless.'

'Ben.'

'Of course — Ben. And please, call me Ingrid.' She frowned, suddenly worried, said, 'You won't say anything to Sven about — ?'

'No,' Lawless said. 'Not a word.'

18

After breakfast, Lawless helped Sven nail down the loose boards in the barn. A few had rotted beyond repair. With no spare wood available to replace them and Sven's credit in Santa Rosa all dried up, Lawless suggested they use the fencing from one of the two corrals, keeping the other intact for the horses. Sven was delighted by the idea and they soon had enough wood to repair not only walls of the barn, but a small leak in the roof as well. 'By golly,' he exclaimed when they were finished. 'Will Ingrid be surprised when she sees what we've done!' He slapped Lawless on the back, adding: 'We make a great team, you and me.'

Lawless grinned, warmed by the big Norwegian's enthusiasm. He couldn't remember the last time he'd felt as happy and relaxed as he did now. But at the same time he knew it couldn't last, not with the way he felt about Ingrid, and he warned himself not to get too comfortable or content.

After they finished repairing the roof, they climbed down to the hayloft and collected all the old junk that Sven sheepishly admitted he had hidden there so Ingrid wouldn't know he hadn't thrown it away like she'd insisted. Among the items were a pitchfork with two prongs missing, a rusted saw with no handle, a surveyor's tripod with only one leg, and an old harness, its leather so deteriorated it broke when they tried to untangle it. 'Heaven only knows why I kept all this stuff,' he said. 'I knew I'd never use it when I was hiding it here. Guess I'm just a pack rat, like Ingrid says.'

'I'm the opposite,' Lawless said. 'I get rid of things too quickly.' Including people, he thought.

'I inherited the trait from my father,' Sven said as they carried the junk out behind the barn. ''Possessions', he used to say, 'are like memories, to be stored away and cherished later'. My mother, on the other hand, was like you. 'Out with the old, in with the new', was her motto.' He chuckled, adding, 'Caused some dreadful arguments. 'The Battling Bjorkmans' they were known as.' He paused, saddened by the thought of his parents, then said, 'I still miss them, Ben. I miss my brothers and sisters, too. I tried to get them to come to America with me, but they wouldn't. Said they loved Norway too much to leave. Thank heavens I have Ingrid and Raven or my life wouldn't be worth a tinker's damn.'

Lawless felt a tinge of guilt, but said nothing.

Returning inside the barn, they lugged an old straw mattress up to the loft for Lawless to sleep on and then stabbed the hay with pitchforks to get rid of any rats. As they worked, Sven asked Lawless if he had a wife and children. Lawless shook his head. How about parents, brothers or sisters? Again, Lawless shook his head. Sven smiled sympathetically, then broke into a big grin and slapped Lawless on the back. 'Well, now you've got us, my friend. So you'll never be lonely again.'

Lawless knew better. But not wanting to hurt Sven's feelings, he kept silent. Finished in the loft, they descended the ladder and let the horses loose into the corral. Sven then grabbed the grease bucket and two brushes and together they began greasing the axles on the wagon. As they worked, Sven told Lawless about what it was like growing up in a village in Norway. In the middle of the conversation he suddenly stopped and looked at the empty stall behind him. 'All right,' he said sternly, 'you can come out now.'

Lawless looked between the spokes of the nearest wheel and saw Raven emerge from the stall. 'I wasn't doing nothing,' she said defensively.

'Anything,' corrected her father. 'If you were doing nothing, you had to be doing something.'

'I meant I wasn't listening to what

you were saying.'

'You'd better not be. I catch you eavesdropping and I'll spank the fur off you.'

'Have to catch me first.'

'I'll do that too,' Sven said, more amused than angry, 'and then I'll double spank you.' He faked a sudden grab at her, but she was ready and easily eluded him. She made no attempt to run away, though, and Lawless realized this was a game between them. 'What're you doing here anyway?' Sven asked her. 'Aren't you supposed to be helping your mother?'

'Nothing to help her with. That crazy Violet's doing everything. And what she isn't doing, Joey is.' Raven frowned, puzzled. 'I swear, the way they keep following Momma around, asking if they can do this or that, they must love doing chores.'

'I doubt that,' her father said. 'They've just been raised properly and want to help out — unlike a certain young lady I know.'

Raven made a face. 'If being a lady means doing chores, I don't want to be one. Are they going to be staying with us from now on?' she added.

'Until they have their own place to live, yes.'

'They got an aunt and uncle in Denver, why don't they go live with them?'

'I've no idea,' Sven said. 'Why, don't you like having them around?'

Raven shrugged. 'I liked it better without them.'

'Really? I figured you'd love their company. They're almost your age, and when Joey's better you and he can do things together. Then you won't have to amuse yourself all day, or spend so much time at the reservation.'

'I like being at the reservation,' Raven said. 'And I like being by myself even better.' She took her slingshot from her back pocket and stretched the rubber strands. 'There's rabbits feeding back of the barn. Want me to kill one or two for supper?'

'So long as you have no chores to do, yes.'

Raven, already halfway to the door, stopped and looked at Lawless. 'That gunfighter you know — one who shot the sheriff?'

'Latigo Rawlins? What about him?' Lawless said.

'I seen him this morning 'fore sunup.'

'Saw him, saw him,' Sven corrected.

'Where?' said Lawless.

'Greenwater Canyon.'

'That's in the hills east of here,' Sven said for Lawless' benefit. 'Half of it's on our property and the other half belongs to the Morgans — or did before the bank stepped in. What was he doing?' he asked Raven.

'I don't know. Didn't ask him.'

'Did he see you?' Lawless said.

'Uh-uh. He was breaking camp when I come up on him. I watched him for a spell and after he'd saddled up, he started climbing over some rocks, you know, like he was looking for something. Then he rode off.'

Sven frowned at Lawless. 'Wonder what he was looking for?'

Lawless shrugged, and turned to Raven. 'Where was he headed?'

'Santa Rosa, looked like. Want me to show you where I saw him?'

Lawless looked questioningly at Sven.

'Go ahead,' he said. 'I'd like to know what Rawlins was up to myself. Oh, and take the horses. That way, you'll be back in time for lunch.'

* * *

It was a twenty-minute ride to Greenwater Canyon, so named because of the green-tinted water in the creek that flowed out of the steep rocky bluffs on either side. Lawless reined up in front of the narrow rock-strewn entrance, unhooked the safety strap that held his Colt in the holster and motioned for Raven to ride behind him. Obeying, she asked what was worrying him. When he didn't answer, she said: 'You think Mr Rawlins doubled back?'

'Possible.'

'You worried he might bushwhack you?'

'Possible.'

'But you're his friend. Why would he shoot — ?'

Lawless reined up and looked back at her. 'Let's get something straight: Latigo's not my friend. He's not anybody's friend.'

'Then why'd he give you your gun back?'

'To prove he wasn't taking orders from the sheriff. It's a sore point with him — like being called Shorty. Both things make him loco.'

'Mean crazy?'

'In a deadly way. As for why he'd shoot me, Lefty doesn't need a reason. With him killing's like an itch. When he itches, he scratches. Simple as that.'

She looked at him suspiciously. 'You ain't making all this up, are you?'

'I couldn't be more serious.' He rode on, Raven right behind him.

They followed the creek as it curved

between rocks and boulders that ancient landslides had brought tumbling down from the hillsides. Lawless did not turn his head but under the flat brim of his black Stetson his eyes were constantly moving, searching the rocky slopes for any sign of danger. Ahead, a dead piñon tree, bleached white by the sun, lay across the creek like a natural bridge.

'Here,' Raven said, reining up by the tree. 'This is where I saw him.'

Lawless dismounted, waited for her to join him and then told her to show him exactly what she saw Latigo doing. Head down as if looking for something, she walked over the broken rocks and loose shale piled alongside the creek.

Lawless followed her. 'Did you see him stop anywhere or pick up any rocks?'

'No . . . Maybe . . . I don't remember.'

'An Apache would remember.'

Raven thought back, face screwed into a frown. 'Once, I think. Over there.' She pointed at some nearby rocks.

Lawless led her to them. 'You're sure it was here?'

'Y-yes. I mean . . . I . . . ' Uncertain, she threw up her hands. 'It isn't fair. I'm just a kid, you know. Can't expect me to remember everything.'

Lawless grasped her arm and pulled her close until their faces were only inches apart. 'Don't play that weak sister game with me. You want to be treated like an adult, act like one.'

Raven glared at him. She pointed at the ground. 'He stopped here, picked up a rock, turned it over in his hand then threw it away and kept looking. I'm sure of it.'

'That's better.' Lawless hunkered down and dipped his hand in the cold, fast-moving greenish water. He scooped up a handful of sandy silt from the creek-bed, examined it then dropped it back in the water.

'Ain't no gold here, if that's what you're looking for.'

Lawless, deep in thought, ignored her.

'No silver, neither.'

Lawless picked up a small, sharp-edged rock that at some time or other a man-made tool had split apart. Examining it, he then thoughtfully tossed it from hand to hand. 'Ever see any prospectors here?'

'Not any more.'

'When?'

'Four, five years ago. Miners mostly, from up around Silver City. Pa said they came here after their mines played out.'

'Your father let them dig on his land?'

'Only if they agreed to give him a share of what they found. But they never found anything. Here or upstream on the Morgans' property. 'Least, nothing that made them keep on digging.'

Lawless filed away the information. 'We're done here,' he said. Mounting, he nudged his horse into a walk and let it pick its own way out of the canyon. He deliberately didn't look back but could hear Raven's horse following, its hoofs ringing sharply on the loose shale.

Once they were clear of the canyon, Raven rode alongside Lawless. She didn't say anything but every now and then he noticed her looking at him. It was a probing look, as if she was trying to figure out what made him tick. He let it slide for a mile or so then said, 'If something's chewing on you, spit it out.'

She didn't answer right away. But just when he thought she had decided not to respond, she said: 'You like my mother, don't you?'

Hiding his surprise, he said casually, 'Yep.'

'No, I mean you *really* like her.'

He looked at her, trying to read her eyes to see if he could figure out where this was leading. But Raven's dark, innocent gaze gave no inkling of what she was thinking and finally Lawless faced front, saying, 'Your ma's a fine generous woman. Gentle and kind, too. Be hard not to like her.'

Raven laughed like she'd uncovered a secret.

'What's so funny?'

'You. Acting like you don't really care when all along you do, you like her a lot, much more than you're saying. I know you do 'cause I seen the way you look at her.'

Deciding this should go no further, he leaned over and grabbed her reins, at the same time reining up so that both horses came to an abrupt halt.

'What're you trying to say?'

His look scared her. She realized she wasn't dealing with her father, a gentle loving man whom she adored, but with a stranger, a man she knew nothing about, a man whose cold, pale-amber stare warned her that he was capable of killing her and riding off without a trace of pity or guilt. Her bravado and truculent insolence, normally a wall of insulation behind which she hid, melted, leaving her naked and alone; vulnerable.

'N-nothing,' she stammered. 'I mean I think it's nice you like her. Momma needs a friend. She's always worrying about someone else, me or Pa or our neighbors, and now Violet and Joey, never herself, and sometimes it wears on her, I know it does 'cause I've heard her crying, especially when she thinks she's alone and . . . and — ' Suddenly she was crying herself, great wrenching sobs that shook her whole body.

Lawless waited, trying to decide if this scrawny little girl who looked like a boy was putting on an act to gain his sympathy, or if he had truly upset her. Sensing it was the latter he pulled her horse close, intending to soothe her. But he couldn't find the right words. Angry with himself, he rested his hand on her shoulder and squeezed reassuringly.

It took a few minutes but finally Raven stopped crying. Lawless removed his hand and smiled at her. 'Time we were getting back, sprout.'

Raven nodded and dried her eyes with her fists. Then, kicking her horse into a lope, she rode alongside Lawless. She didn't look at him or say anything for the rest of the ride. But there was new-found respect in her eyes and in her heart she knew that from now on she would trust this tall taciturn man and obey everything he told her to do without question.

19

When they arrived at the ranch Ingrid and Violet were spreading a blue- and white-checkered table cloth over the picnic table in front of the house. A breeze made the heat tolerable and Joey, arm still in a sling but moving more spryly now, kept the cloth from being blown away by weighting the corners with smooth flat rocks.

Once they had all washed up and were seated, Sven thanked the Lord for their food and their blessings and everyone tucked in. There were hard-boiled eggs, cold roast-chicken, mashed potatoes, baked beans, home-baked bread and pitchers of pantry-cool lemonade made, Ingrid announced, by Violet.

Lawless watched Raven, seated opposite, as Ingrid praised Violet and Joey for all their help and saw the resentment building in her eyes. His gaze shifted to Joey. Since returning from the reservation, the boy had been uneasy around him, barely speaking and doing all he could to avoid being alone with him. Now, as he caught Lawless looking at him, Joey quickly looked away and from then on kept his eyes on his plate. Lawless guessed the boy was still angry at him for shooting him, and knowing only time could heal Joey's anger he turned his attention to Ingrid. Head thrown back, hair as gold as wheat in sunshine, she was laughing at something Sven had said. It was a wonderful laugh, spontaneous and musical, and Lawless knew he'd made a mistake by agreeing to stay — even for a few days. He wanted this woman more than he had thought possible, and every moment he was around her made him desire her more.

The sound of horses approaching jarred his thoughts. He, and the others at the table, turned and saw a dozen riders approaching. They were grim, hard-looking men, all armed with rifles and six-guns, and led by a man in an expensive white Stetson on a magnificent all-black stallion.

Lawless instinctively dropped his hand to his Colt. 'You know who they are?' he asked Sven.

Sven nodded, momentarily too surprised to answer. 'That's Mr Stadtlander,' he said finally. 'And the men, they're some of his riders, the Double SS boys. Remember, we were talking about him yesterday. How powerful he was?'

Lawless nodded.

'I don't get it,' Sven said. 'What the devil is he doing out here?'

'Maybe they want to water their horses,' Ingrid said. Turning to Lawless, she added, 'When we first settled here we occasionally saw him and his son, Slade, in Santa Rosa. But then Mr Stadtlander's gout and arthritis got worse and after that we never saw him again.'

'That's Slade riding beside him,' Sven said. 'The man wearing the gray hat, on the buckskin.'

‘And that black horse Mr Stadtlander’s on,’ Violet said, ‘that’s the mean one Joey was talking about.’

Lawless looked at the gleaming black Morgan stallion, admiring its smooth, effortless gait, proudly arched neck and long flowing mane and tail. It was a horse that most men could only dream of owning, one that made all other horses Lawless had seen seem insignificant. Impressed, he studied the man riding it. Stadtlander was short, squat and powerfully built. But Lawless could tell by the way he sat in the saddle, shoulders hunched over and left hand curled unnaturally inward that arthritis was already starting to cripple him. But he was not surrendering easily. Despite the gray streaking his wavy brown hair and gun-fighter’s mustache, his square, jut-jawed face was filled with arrogance and contempt for anyone who stood in his way. This was a man, Lawless knew, who felt he was above the law.

‘Want me to talk to him?’ Lawless asked Sven. ‘See what he wants?’

'Let's both talk to him,' Sven said, rising. 'But keep an eye on Slade. He's got a chip on his shoulder and he'll keep prodding you, hoping you'll try to knock it off.'

* * *

Stadtlander signaled for his riders to wait outside the gate. He and his son then rode slowly up to Lawless and Sven, standing in front of the house.

'Afternoon, Mr Bjorkman. I'm Stillman — '

'Stadtlander. Yes, I know, sir.' Sven stepped closer, hand extended toward the cattle baron, and immediately had to jump back as the Morgan nipped at him.

'Damn you,' Stadtlander said, jerking on the reins. 'Mind your manners!' It took him a few moments to control the irascible stallion, but then he leaned down and shook Sven's hand. 'You'll have to forgive Brandy, Mr Bjorkman. I don't get to ride him enough these days and — well, as you can see, he's gotten a tad rambunctious.'

'He's a magnificent animal,' Sven said. 'I'm sure he's well worth the trouble. I don't think we've ever met, sir,' he added.

'We haven't,' said Stadtlander. 'But I've seen you and your lovely wife in Santa Rosa from time to time.' As he was talking he glanced at Lawless, trying to size him up. 'Don't think we've met either, have we, mister?'

Lawless shook his head but offered no greeting.

Unaccustomed to being snubbed Stadtlander frowned, offended. But he knew danger when he saw it and not wanting trouble right now, decided not to press the tall man. Turning back to Sven, he introduced his son, Slade, to the bearded Norwegian. The two men nodded their hellos. Slade was taller and leaner than his father, but had none of the older man's pride or indomitable spirit. Instead, despite all his advantages, he was nothing more than a sour-faced swaggering bully known for beating up whores and drunks.

'You're welcome to water your horses,' Sven told Stadtlander. 'And if you're thirsty, there's plenty of fresh lemonade.'

'Thank you, but water's all we'll need.' Stadtlander nodded to Slade, who gestured for the riders to follow him to the trough near the well.

Stadtlander turned back to Sven. 'I have something to say to the Morgans. Won't take but a minute.' Without waiting for Sven's permission, he rode over to the table. There, tipping his hat politely to Ingrid, Stadtlander smiled at Violet and Joey. 'Remember me?'

Violet nodded. 'You came to our ranch once to talk to my father.'

'That's right. I wanted to buy your spread, but your pa wouldn't hear of it.'

'Is that why you killed him, mister?' Joey said.

'Joey!' Violet said.

Statlander frowned, surprised. 'Why

would I want to kill your pa, son?'

'I don't know,' Joey said. 'I don't know why anyone would. I just know it was only a few days after you spoke to him that someone shot him.'

'I give you my word, son, it was not me who shot your pa.'

'Well, someone did,' Joey said angrily. 'And if it wasn't you, it must have been Sheriff Tishman or Mr Edfors.'

'Joey, be quiet!' Violet said. 'You mustn't say things like that.'

'I can understand your anger,' Stadtlander said. 'Reckon I'd feel the same way. But you're accusing the wrong men. The same night your Pa was shot, fifty of my cows were run off. My foreman followed their tracks to the border. Said the rustlers must've driven them across into Mexico. My guess is they're the same border trash who stopped at your ranch and gunned down your pa. Sound reasonable, son?' he asked when Joey didn't say anything.

Joey shrugged. 'I guess.'

'Glad we agree,' Stadtlander said.

'Mr Edfors and Sheriff Tishman have their faults, like we all do, but they ain't coldblooded killers. You have my word on that.'

Joey and Violet wilted under his fierce-eyed gaze.

But Ingrid didn't. 'What exactly do you want, Mr Stadtlander?'

He looked at her shrewdly. 'I just heard about these two young'uns losing their ranch and having their house burned. I came here to tell them that I never meant for either of those things to happen — '

'You?' Ingrid said, surprised. 'I understood from my husband that it was the bank who evicted them.'

'That's true, ma'am, but since I own the bank — '

'You do?' Violet said. 'But I thought Brian — Mr Edfors owned it.'

'He's the manager,' Stadtlander said. 'And a very fine one he is. But knowing I wished to conclude the transaction, he overstepped what I would call 'the boundaries of decency'. And so did

Sheriff Tishman. For that, little lady, I'm mighty sorry. And though it's too late to change what happened, I want to make amends. I've instructed Mr Edfors to make out a draft to you and your brother for one thousand dollars — '

'A th-thousand dollars?' Violet echoed.

'I know money can't make up for the loss of your home, or replace the many fond memories you must have experienced while growing up there, but it will at least give you a start somewhere else.'

'Thank you, Mr Stadtlander,' Violet began. 'We — '

Lawless cut her off. 'Keep your money, mister.'

Stadtlander swung around in the saddle and glared at him. 'What did you say?'

'I said, keep your money.' Lawless turned to Violet. 'You take his thousand dollars, or any amount he offers you, the court will look upon it as a legal sale and you'll never get your ranch back.'

'I don't understand,' Violet said. 'I thought the bank already owned it.'

'They do — for now. But a hearing might change that.'

'How?'

'When the judge hears all the special circumstances, he may rule differently — perhaps even in your favor.'

Stadtlander, ready to erupt, somehow controlled himself. 'I wouldn't listen to him if I were you, Miss Morgan. He's not a lawyer — '

'I don't have to be a lawyer to smell a thief,' Lawless said.

His words crackled in the hot, dry afternoon air. No one moved.

'Mister,' Stadtlander said, teeth gritted, 'I don't know who you are or why you're sticking your damn nose in this, but as God is my witness, I've hanged men for less than what you just called me.'

'Try hanging me,' Lawless said, 'and your stallion will need a new owner.'

'Ben,' Sven began.

'Hold still,' Lawless told him. He

watched as Slade and the Double SS riders, finished watering their horses, rode up beside Stadtlander.

'Something wrong, Pa?' Slade said.

Still boiling, Stadtlander grimly shook his head.

'I just called him a thief,' Lawless said.

'Y-you what?'

'I just called your father a thief.'

Slade and the Double SS riders froze, unable to believe the gall of the tall stranger standing before them. Then:

'You're a dead man,' Slade said.

'Prove it,' Lawless said.

Slade, about to draw, looked into Lawless's narrowed amber eyes and lost his nerve.

Behind him the Double SS riders looked away, disgusted.

Stadtlander, sensing his son was a heartbeat from death, said, 'Leave it be, Son.'

'But Pa — '

'I said, leave it be.' He turned to Sven. 'I didn't come here to make trouble, Mr Bjorkman. I came to right a wrong.'

'You came to steal,' Lawless said. Without taking his eyes off Stadtlander or Slade, he said to Sven, 'Next he was going to offer to buy your place.'

'My place? But it isn't for sale.'

'But you are behind on your note, right?'

Sven shifted uncomfortably. 'A little, yeah. But — '

'Tell him,' Lawless said to Stadtlander. 'Explain how you intend to foreclose on his ranch next.'

'Why would I want to do that?'

'Because he owns half of Greenwater Canyon — the half you didn't get when you stole the Morgans' spread.'

'Why the hell would I want a godforsaken hole-in-the-ground like Greenwater Canyon?'

'Chalcopyrite,' Lawless said.

Stadtlander reacted as if he'd been punched.

'What the devil is chalcopy — whatever you called it?' Sven said.

Lawless ignored him. 'Go ahead, Stadtlander,' he said. 'Tell him what chalcopyrite is. And while you're at it, tell Violet and Joey, too. That way, they'll know why you were so 'generously' giving them a thousand dollars.'

Rage bubbling over, Stadtlander stabbed a finger at Lawless. 'My son's right, mister: you *are* a dead man!' He whirled the stallion around, dug his spurs in and galloped away.

Slade threw a curse at Lawless, then he and the Double SS riders rode after Stadtlander.

Lawless, Sven and everyone at the picnic table watched them ride out the gate into the sun-scorched scrubland. Dust soon swallowed them up.

Ingrid rose from the table and joined Lawless and her husband.

'You've made a bad enemy, Ben.'

'Wouldn't be the first,' Lawless said.

'You've also just cost Violet and Joey a thousand dollars. I think you'd best explain yourself.'

Lawless took a small rock from his

denim jacket and placed it on the table in view of everyone. The color of rust, the chalcopyrite ore was sprinkled with pale greenish-blue lumps.

'What're we looking at?' Sven asked.

'Copper,' Lawless said.

20

'Copper?' Sven repeated.

Lawless nodded. 'I'm no geologist, but I know chalcopyrite when I see it. And from the amount I saw scattered along the creek in Greenwater Canyon, I'd say you — and Violet and Joey, here — are standing on a whole mountain of it.'

It took a moment for what he'd said to sink in. Then:

'I've seen pictures of copper mines,' Ingrid said, puzzled. 'They're nothing but enormous man-made craters.'

'Me, too,' Sven said. 'How come this copper's above ground?'

'Earthquakes, most likely,' Lawless said. 'Ancient ones that spewed out huge chunks of it, forming bluffs, and then over time landslides dumped some of the ore into the canyon along the creek. I'm not saying that what's above ground will make you rich,' he added, 'it won't. But if I'm right, what's buried below will.'

'I'll be damned,' Sven said. 'No wonder Mr Stadtlander wants to get his hands on Greenwater Canyon.'

Ingrid said, 'Do you think that's what that gunman — what was his name?'

'Latigo Rawlins, ma'am. And yes, since he works for Stadtlander, I'm sure that's what he was doing there. Lefty's got a smell for money in any form.'

'Oh, Joey!' Violet jumped up and threw her arms around her brother. 'Isn't that wonderful? We might be getting our ranch back.'

'And maybe we'll be rich, too,' Joey said excitedly.

Raven looked at them with mild reproach. 'Ain't you forgetting something?'

'Aren't,' corrected her father. 'Not ain't.'

Raven ignored him. 'Takes money to dig for copper. Lots of money. Mr Stadtlander's got it and we don't.'

'That's not your concern,' Lawless said. 'Once word gets out that there's maybe big copper deposits on your land, you'll have so many offers from mining companies or investors back East to dig it up for you — or to buy the canyon at a price you can't refuse — you'll have to fight them off with pitchforks.'

'And for mining the copper,' Sven said, 'these folks will take a bite out of the profits?'

'A big bite,' Lawless said. 'But there'll still be plenty left over for you — all of you.'

'That's good enough for me.' Sven turned to Violet and Joey. 'How about you two?'

They nodded eagerly. 'Just so we get our ranch back,' Violet said.

'It's all settled then,' said Sven. Leaning close to Ingrid, he whispered something in her ear. She nodded. Sven turned to Lawless, adding, 'If there is copper under our feet, my wife and I want you to share in our profits.'

'Sven, I —'

'No, no, hear me out. You've earned it, my friend. If you hadn't braced Mr Stadtlander the way you did, I never would've known he was after Greenwater Canyon — 'least not until he and the sheriff forced us off our land and by then it would've been too late.'

'And if we do get our ranch back,' Violet said, 'same goes for us, Mr Lawless. Isn't that right, Joey?'

Joey nodded, but would not look at Lawless.

'That's kindly of you,' Lawless said. 'And when the time comes, if I'm still around, we'll talk about it.'

'What do you mean 'if'?' Sven said. 'You'll be around. Who do you think's going to help me turn this place into a horse ranch?'

'What I know about horse ranches,' Lawless said, grinning, 'you could fit into your wife's sewing thimble.'

'So we'll learn together. Better still, become partners. Tell him, sweetheart,'

Sven said to Ingrid. 'Tell him he has to stay.'

'It wouldn't matter what I told him,' she said quietly. 'Ben is a man who makes up his own mind. Isn't that right, Ben?'

'Mostly,' Lawless said, looking at her in a way that suggested she could change his mind.

'So what do we do next?' Violet said.

'I ride to Deming,' Sven said.

'What's in Deming?' Ingrid asked.

'Who not what,' Sven said, adding: 'Jud Halloran, remember?'

'The lawyer?'

'You bet. He always said he'd help us if we ever needed legal advice. Well, now we need it.' Sven turned to Lawless. 'I'll tell Jud what you just told us and see what he says. He's a smart fellow. Maybe he can persuade a judge to listen to our side in court.'

'If he can,' Lawless said, 'make sure he also asks the judge to issue an injunction preventing the bank, or Mr Stadtlander, from taking over Violet and

Joey's ranch — at least until he's reached his decision.'

'I sure will,' Sven said.

'And you'll pay Jud with what,' Ingrid said 'turnips from my vegetable garden?'

All the air seemed to rush out of her husband and he sagged dejectedly.

'If this Halloran's as smart as you say,' Lawless said, 'he'll take the case on contingency.'

'What's that mean?' Joey asked.

'He'll represent you for a percentage of your profits.'

'By golly, that's a wonderful idea!' Sven clapped Lawless warmly on the back. 'See, I told you we were a great team.'

'Let's not get carried away,' Ingrid cautioned. 'We're not mine owners yet.'

'Or rich,' reminded Violet.

'But we're going to be,' Sven said. 'I can feel it in my bones.' He raised his glass of lemonade in toast. 'To copper — and the man who found it for us!'

'Hey, what about me?' Raven said. 'If

I hadn't told you about seeing that gunfighter in the canyon, none of this would have happened.'

'You're right,' her father said. 'Everybody, here's to Miss Smarty Pants.'

They all drank to Raven, who beamed.

'And finally,' Sven said lovingly to Ingrid, 'to you, my wonderful wife, for making every day a blessing.'

Ingrid smiled, a little self-consciously, and lifted her cheek so Sven could bend down and kiss her. 'I love you,' he whispered. 'Love you too,' she whispered back. Sven lingered another moment then he moved on down the table to refill his glass. Ingrid glanced at Lawless.

He stood watching her from nearby. Their gazes held for a moment. Then Ingrid, as if knowing what he was thinking, blushed and looked away.

Lawless waited to see if she would look his way again. When she didn't, and he saw the pink in her cheeks, he faced front — and found Raven standing in his path. She didn't say anything but her large, shining black eyes let him know that she'd seen everything and knew what was going on.

For once though, she didn't say anything smart. She gave him the faintest of smiles, then stepped around him and joined her mother.

Lawless, feeling empty inside, headed for the barn.

Behind him he heard Raven say, 'He's a lot different than Pa, isn't he, Momma?'

'Yes,' Ingrid said. 'They're about as different as two men could get.'

* * *

That night as Lawless stood leaned against the barn door, smoking his last cigarette before turning in, he sensed he was being watched.

'The Apaches taught you well,' he said without turning.

There was an irritated sigh and

Raven appeared out of the darkness.

'Not well enough,' she said. 'You heard me.'

'Uh-uh. Didn't hear a thing.'

'Then how'd you know it was me and not some renegade buck off the reservation?'

Lawless enjoyed a final drag on his cigarette before grinding it out under his heel. 'How many Apaches you know smell of Williams Shaving-Mug Soap?'

'Damn!' Raven stamped her foot in disgust. 'I forgot all about that.'

Lawless chuckled. 'Since when'd you start shaving, sprout?'

'I haven't. It was Pa. I was arguing with him 'bout going into town with Momma tomorrow when of a sudden he reaches out and swipes me with that ol' boar bristle brush of his . . . made me look like I'd dipped my face in buttermilk.'

'Your father's shaving?' Lawless said, surprised.

'Was. Right after supper.'

'What brought that about?'

'Momma's birthday. He does it every year. You know. As his special gift to her.

'Whoa, whoa, tomorrow's your mother's birthday?'

'Uh-huh. That's why I wanted to go into town with her — to get this dress Pa ordered special all the way from St. Louis — '

'But your father's riding to Deming tomorrow.'

'Yeah, and Momma's not too happy about it, I'll tell you. They were arguing over it when I snuck out. Momma wants him to wait one more day, you know, so they can celebrate her birthday together like they've always done ever since they left Norway . . . '

Lawless thought a moment, then said, 'You never told me, all right?'

'Told you what?'

'About your ma's birthday. You never mentioned it. Understand?'

Raven shrugged her bony, tanned shoulders. 'If you say so . . . '

* * *

Sven emerged, yawning, from the house and joined Lawless standing in the darkness a few steps away. He looked lumpy and shapeless in a long flannel nightgown. The lower half of his face was white where his beard had been shaved off. He appeared younger and more civilized and had Lawless passed him in the street, he would not have recognized him. 'What's so important it couldn't wait till morning, Ben?'

'I want you to write a letter introducing me to that lawyer you know in Deming.'

'Jud Halloran? Why?'

'Because I'm going to see him, not you.'

'W-what?'

'I know it's sudden, but I've been thinking about it and there's no doubt in my mind that I should be the one who talks to him. I know much more about this kind of thing than you do, and I'll be able to tell him exactly what we need him — and the judge — to do for you and the Morgans.'

'But — '

'No buts,' Lawless said. 'This is your future we're talking about. You can't risk fouling it up because you didn't give the lawyer all the facts. You can see it makes sense,' he added as Sven started to protest, 'and why it has to be me who goes?'

'But Ben, you already done so much for us — '

'This isn't just about you,' Lawless lied. 'Keep it to yourself, but I have a daughter, about Raven's age, who lives just outside Deming with her mom's folks . . . I haven't seen her in God knows how long and who knows how long it'll be before I see her again. This is my chance to spend some time with her.'

Sven grinned and scratched his naked white chin. 'A daughter,' he said happily. 'By golly, Ben, I knew you couldn't be all by yourself in this world.

I mean it just wasn't natural.'

'I won't take too long,' Lawless said.

'You take as long as you like, my friend, y'hear? Day, two days — a week if need be. Hell's bells, you ol' dog, bring her back here if you want. We'll make her welcome, you know we will.'

'Thanks,' Lawless said. 'I might do that. Now you go write that letter while I'll saddle up. Sooner I get to Deming and explain everything to Mr Halloran, sooner I can see my daughter.'

'I'll have Ingrid pack you some grub,' Sven said. 'There's nothing but desert and rattlers 'tween here and Deming. Oh, and I'll give you an extra canteen just in case — ' He suddenly broke off and chuckled.

'What?' said Lawless.

'Ingrid . . . she's going to jump for joy when I tell her you're going instead of me.'

'She dislikes me that much?'

'Dislikes? No, no, she thinks the world of you — she and Raven both.

But tomorrow's her birthday and I bought her a mail-order dress a while back. It's just sitting there in Melvin's Haberdashery, waiting to be picked up.'

'That's great,' Lawless said. 'Then this will work out fine.'

'Couldn't be better,' Sven said. He hurried into the house.

Lawless stood there a moment, insects whining about his ears, looking at the curtained window. A light appeared as Sven lit the lamp. Lawless saw his bear-like silhouette moving around beyond the curtain as he searched for paper and pen. Another shadow joined him. It was smaller and slimmer, but too big for Raven, and Lawless guessed it was Ingrid.

He sighed heavily. Then cursing himself for being a damned fool, he wondered what it would have been like to have spent two whole days with Ingrid without her husband around.

The thought made him long for her even more and, as he walked to the barn, he wondered if after he'd finished his business with the lawyer, he oughtn't to keep riding west and never come back this way again.

21

It was early morning when Lawless rode into Deming.

Originally shunned by settlers because it was home to numerous outlaw gangs and frequently attacked by marauding Apaches, the dusty, sun-baked town had become prominent once the Atchison, Topeka and the Santa Fe completed its junction with the Southern Pacific railroad in 1881. Named after Mary Deming Crocker, wife of the railroad magnate Charles Crocker, it had finally shed its bad image and become a safe place to live with gas street lights, hotels, stores, cantinas, law offices and one of the most elegant Harvey Houses west of St Louis.

Lawless rode along Silver Avenue, a broad dirt street lined on both sides with planked sidewalks and wood and brick buildings, looking for a place to water his horse. There were water windmills everywhere, reminding him of the town's nickname: Windmill City.

Near the end of the street Lawless saw Jud Halloran's shingle hanging above a stairway leading up to his office. Guessing the lawyer wouldn't be open for business at this early hour, he rode on. At the next corner he passed the Baker Hotel, an impressive two-storey brick building that was Deming's most important meeting place. Lawless crossed Spruce Street and reined up outside a large livery stable with mission-style parapets and a decorative brick front.

There was a public water trough by the entrance. Lawless dismounted and stretched the stiffness from his back while his horse drank. Then, taking the hardboiled egg sandwiches Ingrid had fixed for him from his saddle-bag, he sat on the edge of the trough to eat. She had also given him two oatmeal cookies and after wolfing everything down Lawless went to the pump, cranked it and drank from the spout.

As he straightened up he noticed the hostler watching him from the doorway of the barn. He was an old, bald man with a snuff-stained white beard who leaned on a crutch and had a splint on his right leg. ''Morning,' he said to Lawless. 'Just git in?'

Lawless nodded. Then thanking the hostler for the use of his water, he asked him if he knew what time Mr Halloran opened his office. The hostler shrugged and said it all depended on how hungry the lawyer was. Taking out an old silver timepiece, he snapped open the cover and checked the time. ''Course, if you're on fire to see him, mister, reckon you can catch him wolfing down flapjacks right about now.'

'Where would that be?' Lawless said.

The hostler pointed up the street. 'Oro Fino, on Railroad Avenue 'cross from the railroad tracks.'

Thanking the old man, Lawless stepped into the saddle and nudged his horse on up the street.

* * *

Thanks to simple, wholesome food at reasonable prices — reasonable when compared to the price of meals served at the large, fancy Harvey House next to the train station — the wood-framed, family-owned restaurant was always crowded with railroad men, drummers, and cattlemen.

Entering, Lawless stood just inside the door and searched the faces of the customers, looking for a man fitting Sven's description. He spotted him quickly, a big chunky man with thinning dark hair and long sideburns in a tan business suit sitting at a rear corner table.

'Mr Halloran?'

Jud Halloran waved him away without looking up, 'Not now,' and continued forking syrupy pancakes into his mouth.

'It's important,' Lawless said.

'So's my breakfast,' Halloran said with his mouth full. When Lawless didn't move the lawyer finally looked up, patted his mouth with a napkin and pointed to a clock on the wall. 'I'll be in my office in thirty minutes. We can talk then.' He returned to his eating.

Lawless took out Sven's letter of introduction and set it on the table beside Halloran's plate. 'Maybe you should read this,' he said.

Halloran glanced at it and was about to continue eating when he saw Sven's signature at the bottom of the page. 'I'll be damned,' he said. Putting his fork down, he gave Lawless a friendlier look and then indicated the chair across from him. 'Join me, Mr Lawless. Coffee?'

'Thanks.'

Halloran turned in his chair and motioned to a waitress serving three grimy, bearded miners at a nearby table. Rather than shout above the noise of everyone talking, he pointed to Lawless and then held up his coffee cup. The waitress nodded to show she understood and headed for the counter.

Halloran turned back to Lawless and sized him up with shrewd, glittery eyes. 'So you're a friend of Sven Bjorkman's, eh? How is that big lumbering ox, anyway — still as cheerful as ever?'

Lawless nodded. He'd already decided he didn't like Halloran and was puzzled that Sven was associated with him.

'And Ingrid — how's she doing?'

'Fine.'

'By God, sir, that is one handsome, lusty, desirable woman, wouldn't you agree?'

Lawless considered knocking Halloran across the room, but managed to restrain himself.

'To this day,' the lawyer continued, 'I hate to think of her rotting away in the desert, getting old and ugly before her time. I told her that when they were passing through. Said she and Sven ought to settle here. I even offered to put her to work in my office at good wages. But she'd have none of it. Said she was determined to help her husband raise horses. I could see she thought the sun rose and set on Sven, so I didn't try to change her mind . . .' He paused, gave a disgusted grunt as if he'd let a prize escape him and then said, 'Ah, well, that was then, this is now. No good crying over spilled cream, is there?' Belching behind his napkin, he pushed his plate away, took a cigar from a leather cigar case, cut off the tip with a gold clipper and slowly wet the end between his lips. He then flared a match, lit up and peered at Lawless through exhaled smoke. 'All right, Mr Lawless, what's this about?'

Lawless started to explain, but as soon as he mentioned Stadtlander's name Halloran cut him off.

'Wait — hold it right there. Before you go any further, Mr Lawless, does the reason you're here, talking to me, have anything to do with Mr Stillman Stadtlander?'

'Everything,' Lawless said. 'And none of it's good.'

'Well, then, I have to tell you, sir, we

have a conflict of interests here. You see, I represent Mr Stadtlander — '

'You're his lawyer?'

'One of many, yes.' Halloran paused as the waitress arrived. Setting a cup of coffee in front of Lawless, she asked if he wanted to order breakfast. When he shook his head, she gathered up Halloran's empty dishes and took them into the kitchen.

'So you can see, can't you,' Halloran continued, 'I'd be violating the law if I represented you or Sven as well.'

Lawless sipped his coffee and studied the lawyer over the cup. 'How long you been in his employ?'

'I'm not at liberty to reveal that, Mr Lawless.' He got up from the table, adding, 'Now, if there's nothing else I can do for you, sir, I have to be getting along.'

'Sit down,' Lawless said, so softly he could barely be heard above the customers talking around them.

But Halloran heard. He heard and he sat quickly.

'How about another lawyer, Mr Halloran?'

'You mean someone I'd recommend?'

Lawless nodded.

'I'm afraid I don't know any other lawyers.'

'You mean none that would risk a face-off with Mr Stadtlander?'

Halloran smiled condescendingly. 'Those are your words, sir, not mine. Now, I really must go.' Rising, he threw money on the table for the meal and hurried out.

Lawless finished his coffee and left the restaurant.

There were two other lawyers in Deming. Both were suddenly 'too busy' to listen to Lawless once he mentioned Stadtlander's name. They added 'confidentially' that they doubted if any of the local judges would rule against Mr Stadtlander even if Mr Bjorkman was lucky enough to find a lawyer to represent him.

Angry and frustrated, Lawless watered

his horse at the livery stable, filled both his canteens and rode out of town. It was almost noon and the sun hammered down on him. He dozed in the saddle for a while, in no rush to get back to the ranch and give Sven the bad news, and finally decided to rest up until sundown. Finding a sliver of shade beside a rocky outcrop, he removed his saddle, hobbled the horse, and stretched out on the warm sand.

He was asleep within moments.

22

A silver dollar moon guided him back to the ranch. But as he dismounted outside the barn, the moon ducked behind the clouds and it became dark, so dark he had to light the lamp hanging by the door in order to put the horse away.

The other horse was missing. Puzzled, Lawless went out back and saw that the wagon was also missing. Yet a light glowed in the window of the house. Someone was home. He walked down the slope to the front door. It wasn't much past supper but he couldn't hear anyone talking inside. It made him uneasy and he sensed something was terribly wrong. He rapped on the door. 'It's me, Ben,' he called out. When no one responded he knocked again, harder. 'Sven . . . Ingrid . . . it's Ben . . . Ben Lawless . . . '

Still no answer.

Fears escalating, he drew his Colt, opened the door and stepped inside.

The room was empty. Still. Silent.

Then he heard a faint tapping that drew his eyes to the hurricane lamp on the table. A Miller moth hurled itself repeatedly against the glass shield protecting the wick. The charred remains of another moth lay near the flame.

Hoping that the moth was the only dead creature he was going to find, Lawless cautiously entered the back bedrooms. They were also empty. Holstering his gun, he returned to the main room and looked around. There was no sign of violence anywhere. He put his hand on the stove. It was cold. Not wanting to be a target, he blew out the lamp and inched open the door.

Nothing stirred.

Somewhere far off a coyote sang in the night.

Lawless stepped outside. He stood there, looking around, trying to see in the darkness, ready to dive back inside if there was any trouble.

The moon now slid from behind the clouds, turning everything silvery bright. He looked about him. There were no signs of an attack by renegades, white or red. Everything looked undisturbed, as if the ranch had suddenly been abandoned. A cold wind blew in from the desert. It spun the vanes of the windmill and their creaking made him look up.

That's when he saw a figure slumped over on the little platform just below the vanes. He moved closer and realized it was Raven, knees drawn up, face buried in her arms.

'What the hell you doing up there?' he called out to her.

She showed no sign of hearing him.

'Raven — you hear me? Where is everybody?'

Again, she didn't respond.

Hurrying to the windmill, he climbed up the rickety ladder until his head and shoulders were above the platform. Raven still didn't move. Not wanting to add his weight to the flimsy structure, he reached out and gently grasped her arm. 'What's wrong, sprout? Why won't you talk to me?'

After a long pause, she said tearfully, ' 'S'all her fault . . . '

He knew she wasn't finished, so he remained quiet.

'If she hadn't kept after him about it . . . made him take her into town for that stupid dress, he'd still be alive.'

Lawless felt a chill that wasn't the wind. 'Who would?'

'Pa.'

'Your father's dead?'

Raven nodded.

'When? How?'

Raven lifted her head and looked at him, her big black eyes raw from crying. 'Yesterday morning, in Santa Rosa . . . just after Momma and me had come out of the store . . . '

'Go on.'

'Pa was still inside, talking to Mr and Mrs Melvin . . . when suddenly there was all this shooting and hollering and everybody started running . . . you know, taking cover, ducking into doorways . . . hiding behind wagons, and then, then the three of them came riding up from Lower Front Street — '

'Which three?' Lawless said. 'Who're you talking about?'

'Mr Stadtlander's son, Slade.'

'Who else?'

'The Iverson brothers . . . hired hands who work for Mr Stadtlander. They'd all been drinking at the Copper Palace when — '

'What about Violet and Joey — where were they?'

'Over at the McNallys'.'

'Your neighbors?'

Raven nodded. 'We dropped them off on our way into Santa Rosa. It was Mrs McNally's idea. She and Mr McNally were old friends of Violet's folks . . . '

A gust of wind hit the windmill, cranking the vanes so violently the platform shuddered. Raven gave a tiny gasp and clutched Lawless' arm. He waited until the wind died down and the windmill stopped swaying and then pulled her toward him. She resisted momentarily. Then when he told her to relax, to trust him, she crawled to him and let him help her down the ladder. Once on the ground, he picked her up and carried her into the house.

Sitting her at the table, he lit the lamp and took a half-empty bottle of whiskey from a cupboard beside the pantry. Pouring a little in a cup, he insisted she drink it. He then sat across from her and swigged from the bottle as she finished her story.

Hearing all the wild shooting, she said, her father came running out of Melvin's Haberdashery to see who was doing it. Just then Slade and the Iversons galloped past, guns in one hand and whiskey bottles in the other. They were whooping it up and firing at everything in sight. Bullets flew in all directions. One shattered the store display window behind her mother. Glass showered over them. Her father shouted for them to get back inside.

But bullets kept them pinned down. Finally he grabbed them and tried to pull them into the store. But before he could he was hit by one of the bullets. He staggered backward, blood pouring from his head, and collapsed on the boardwalk. By then, Raven continued, Slade and the Iversons had stopped shooting and ridden on up the street. She and her mother tried to pick her father up, but he was too heavy for them. Her mother screamed for help, but everyone was too scared or busy hiding to answer her cries. Eventually, Mr Melvin and his assistant, Aaron Brock, rushed out of the store and between all of them they were able to carry her father to the doctor's.

'What happened then?' Lawless said as Raven paused.

'... P-Pa ... died ...'

Lawless felt a rare sense of loss. He tried to squelch it. But the feeling fought him and reaching across the table, he gently pressed his hand over Raven's. 'I'm sorry ...'

He expected her to break down, to burst into tears. But she was all cried out. She sat there, motionless, numbly staring at the lamp.

He said quietly, 'What about your mother? Why isn't she here with you?' When Raven avoided his gaze, he added, 'Is she still in Santa Rosa?'

'Y-yes . . . with Mr and Mrs Melvin. They made us stay. Said we shouldn't be out here all alone — '

'But you ran off and left her?'

Her guilty look confirmed it.

'Want to tell me why?'

''Cause it's her fault Pa's dead,' Raven said hotly.

'That's crazy talk.'

'No it ain't. If she hadn't made Pa go into town he'd still be alive. Her and her stupid dumb dress! Who cares if it came all the way from St. Louis? I don't. And neither does — *did* Pa and . . . and now he's dead and I h-hate Momma for it! Hate her . . . hate . . . ' She buried her face in her arms.

Rising, he came and rested his hands

on her shoulders. 'Sprout, listen to me. I know you're hurting right now. And you got a right to. But hating your mother for something that wasn't her fault won't get rid of the pain. People die. Good people, bad people. I don't know why. It's just God's way. If he puts your name on a bullet it'll find you no matter where you are.'

'What's that supposed to mean?'

'That when it's your turn to die, you die. Like your pa. If he'd stayed home yesterday or ridden to Deming instead of me, it wouldn't have made any difference. He still would've died — wherever he was — just in a different way.'

Raven looked up angrily. 'How do you know? You ain't God.'

'No, but I've seen enough death to know how God works.'

'You're just saying that 'cause you love Momma and don't want me to blame her.'

'No,' he said quietly, 'I'm saying it because it's true.'

'I don't believe you. I'll never believe you.'

'Then believe this . . .' He unbuttoned his shirt, revealing the ugly rope scar around his neck. 'What other reason could there be for me being alive?'

Raven grimaced and quickly turned away. She made no sound, but he felt her shoulders shaking and knew she was crying. He wanted to help her, to make her feel better, but he knew only time could do that. Bending down, he gently scooped her up and carried her into her bedroom.

She didn't fight him; didn't even look at him. Her black, normally expressive eyes were empty. Putting her on the bed he covered her with a blanket and pulled a chair up beside her. The room was dark save for a shaft of light coming from the lamp in the other room. Lawless pulled the door almost shut, making the bedroom darker, and sat in the chair.

When his eyes grew accustomed to

the darkness he saw she was staring blankly at the ceiling.

'Go to sleep, sprout.'

She turned her empty eyes to him.

'It's OK,' he assured her. 'I'm not going anywhere.'

She looked at him for another moment. Then she turned on her side facing him and closed her eyes.

Lawless shifted on the hard wooden chair, trying to get comfortable.

Instantly she opened her eyes, anxiously looking for him.

'Don't worry. I'm still here.'

She hesitated, afraid to close her eyes.

'Trust me, sprout. I won't leave you.'

'Why should I trust you?'

He leaned close. 'Look in my eyes. What do you see?' he said when she obeyed.

'Nothing.'

'Look deeper.'

She did, squinting to see better in the dimness.

'What do you see now?'

Raven frowned, puzzled by what she saw, and said, 'I don't know . . . can't explain it. But whatever it is it makes me feel good, you know like . . . like you'd never hurt me . . . that I'm safe with you . . . just like the way I felt when I was with you in Greenwater Canyon. Is that what trust is?' she added. 'Feeling safe when you're with somebody?'

'Close enough,' he said.

She was getting sleepy now and had to fight to keep her eyes open. 'How . . . 'bout you?'

'How about me, what?'

'You ever trust someone?'

About to say no, he realized that would have been a lie and instead said, 'Once.'

'Who . . . was . . . that?'

'Your pa.' He leaned over her and gently brushed her eyes shut with his cupped hand. 'Now, how about going to sleep for me?'

Raven murmured something he didn't catch. Then, exhausted, she let all her fears go in a long sigh and went to sleep.

Lawless took out the makings, built himself a smoke, flared a match to it and prepared himself for a long sleepless night.

23

The next morning, after a breakfast neither felt like eating, they rode double into Santa Rosa. The streets were empty. But an angry crowd was gathered outside the old clapboard courthouse. Most of them were shouting and brandishing their fists at Sheriff Forbes and his four deputies who stood on the steps in front of the entrance, refusing to let any more people inside.

Lawless reined up beside a man at the rear of the crowd and asked him what was going on. Judge Kragen was holding an emergency hearing, the man said, to determine who shot Sven Bjorkman. Of course everyone in town knew it was either Slade Stadtlander or one of the Iversons and wanted the culprit hanged for it. But Mr Stadtlander's lawyer insisted that since no one could prove conclusively who had fired the actual bullet that killed Sven that meant there was a 'reasonable doubt' about the shooter's identity. Therefore, by law, his clients must be considered innocent and should not be charged with a crime.

Lawless bit back his anger and asked how the judge had responded. The man looked surprised that Lawless would ask such an absurd question. Judge Kragen, he said, naturally agreed with the lawyer and said it would definitely influence his decision. That infuriated all the folks who wanted Slade and the Iversons brought to justice and several of them jumped up and accused the judge of playing favorites. Outraged, Judge Kragen banged his gavel on the desk and yelled 'Order in the court, order in the court!' Then he threatened to clear the courtroom if they didn't quiet down. But that only made everyone angrier and later, after several more outbursts, the judge finally ordered the deputies to escort the unruly mob out.

'What about Momma?' Raven said. 'The judge didn't make her leave, did he?'

'No, no, she had nothing to do with it. Fact is, other than when she told the judge her side of what happened during the shooting, your ma never said two words. She just sat there in a sort of daze, twisting her handkerchief around her fingers and looking mighty sad.'

'How about old man Stadtlander,' Lawless said, 'was he in the courtroom?'

'Sure. Sitting right in the front row behind his lawyer. Had himself a fair piece to say, too.'

'About what?'

'Mostly, how folks in town were jealous of what he'd accomplished and were taking their hatred for him out on his son. People began booing him. But he ignored them and said that the citizens of Santa Rosa were treating his boy unfairly . . . always accusing him of being drunk and causing trouble . . .

when in fact Slade was just high-spirited and, like any young man, only trying to have a little harmless fun. 'Course, that got everyone even more riled up. They called Mr Stadtlander a bunch of names you can't say in church and when the judge ordered them to pipe down, they turned on him, calling him corrupt and saying he was nothing but a puppet dancing to Mr Stadtlander's tune and, and that's when he kicked 'em all out.'

'Then what happened?' Lawless said.

'I don't know,' the man said. 'I'm proud to say I was one of the folks the judge kicked out.' Turning to Raven, he added: 'I'm mighty sorry 'bout your pa, little lady. There wasn't a kinder or more giving man in the whole territory. I mean, heck, last year right afore the big snow come, if he hadn't helped me put a new roof on my cabin when Ellie was with child, we would have surely froze to death.' Respectfully tipping his hat, he rejoined his friends.

Hitching their horse to a tie-rail, Lawless led Raven through the crowd and up to the courthouse entrance. Immediately the deputies barred their way and the sheriff ordered them to get off the steps.

Lawless refused to move. 'Raven has a right to be in the courtroom,' he insisted. 'She's Mrs Bjorkman's daughter.'

'I know who she is,' the sheriff said.

'Then let us through.'

'I can't. No one's allowed in till the hearing's over. Judge Kragen's orders. I'm sorry about your pa,' he added to Raven. 'He was a fine man. We're all going to miss him.'

'Then why don't you hang the weasels who killed him?' she said.

Sheriff Lonnie Forbes, a tall, big-bellied man, solemnly stroked his gray waxed mustache. 'Who gets hanged and who don't ain't up to me, missy. That's Judge Kragen's decision. And right now, His Honor is trying to establish exactly what happened.'

'Everybody already knows what happened,' Raven said angrily. 'If you don't believe me, ask them.' She thumbed at the crowd. 'They all saw Slade and the Iversons riding around, shooting at everything.'

'She's right,' shouted a man. 'I was in Sam's getting a shave when the three of 'em rode past, lead flying everywhere.'

'Drunken bastards!' yelled another. 'They ought to be hanged!'

'Somebody get a rope!' said a third man.

'All right, that's enough!' Sheriff Forbes swung his shotgun down off his shoulder, thumbed the hammers back and aimed at the crowd. 'Next one of you jaspers says anything 'bout ropes or lynching, he'll cool off in jail. As for you two,' he said to Lawless and Raven, 'get off these steps. Now!'

Grudgingly, Lawless and Raven obeyed.

* * *

They didn't have long to wait. The sun had barely cleared the cross atop the old mission-style church when the courthouse doors swung open and the townspeople who'd been listening to the hearing came pouring out. They were quickly surrounded by the crowd, all anxious to hear the outcome of the hearing.

Everyone tried to speak at once. Finally one man quieted the crowd and explained what had happened. The judge had declared Slade and the Iverson brothers innocent! All charges had been dropped due to insufficient evidence! Despite killing an innocent bystander, a man loved by everybody, the three drunken shooters were free as jay birds!

The crowd erupted. Everyone surged forward, some of them angrily pumping their fists and others hurling clods of dirt at the courthouse, all demanding that Judge Kragen reconsider.

The deputies held their ground, but hesitated to open fire on their friends and neighbors.

Sheriff Forbes quickly stepped forward and fired his shotgun into the air. The thundering blast jarred the crowd back to reality. Everyone immediately stopped shouting and fell back.

'All right, that's enough,' the sheriff said. 'It's all over. Go home! All of you! Go on!' he added when a few people lingered. 'You got no business here anymore. Unless you want to be arrested, get moving. *Pronto*!'

Reluctantly, everyone dispersed.

Everyone but Lawless and Raven.

'You heard me, mister,' Sheriff Forbes said. 'Git.'

Lawless didn't move. Below the brim of his black hat his eyes were two yellow slits. 'Don't press me, Sheriff,' he warned.

Sheriff Forbes glared at the tall, implacable man standing before him. 'Is that a threat?'

'Call it what you want,' Lawless said. 'But we're not moving till her mother comes out.'

The sheriff frowned, surprised by the

stranger's defiance. There were five shotguns pointed at him and yet he appeared unfazed by them. He just stood there, inflexible, his calm, fearless confidence making the sheriff feel uneasy. The lawman sweated it out for a few moments, then wilted and said to the nearest deputy, 'Utley, go tell Mrs Bjorkman her daughter's waiting for her.'

The deputy hurried inside.

The sheriff, trying to regain his swagger, turned back to Lawless. 'You took a mighty big risk, mister. Hadn't been for young Raven standing next to you, you would've eaten a load of buckshot.'

Lawless smiled, a thin smile that never reached his eyes. 'Then I reckon you can consider yourself a lucky man.'

'Why's that?'

'You wouldn't have lived to see it.'

Sheriff Forbes reddened and his jaw muscles bulged as he gritted his teeth. His finger tightened on the trigger of his shotgun. A shootout seemed inevitable. Then caution overrode his anger and lowering the gun, he said to Lawless, 'I'm a patient man, mister. But if I ever see you in Santa Rosa again, so help me God, I'll find a reason to arrest you.' Motioning for his deputies to follow, he stormed down the steps.

Raven watched the lawmen march across the street to the sheriff's office, then turned to Lawless. 'You sure don't go out of your way to make friends, do you?'

Lawless smiled and playfully tousled her hair. 'Just taking a page out of your book, sprout.'

The courthouse door swung open and Ingrid stepped out. Swathed in black, she looked haggard and puffy-eyed from crying. But on seeing Raven she sagged with relief and quickly embraced her. 'Oh, sweetheart, I'm so glad to see you. Are you all right?'

Raven nodded, and sullenly pulled away from her mother.

'You shouldn't have run off like that,'

Ingrid scolded. 'I was worried sick about you.'

'No reason to be. I was at home.'

'How was I supposed to know that? My God, you could have been dead for all I knew.'

'Wish I was,' Raven said.

'Raven!' Ingrid recoiled as if struck. 'That's a dreadful thing to say.'

'It's true. Then I'd be with Pa.'

'Oh, child, how can you be so hurtful?'

''Cause I hate — '

'That's enough!' Lawless stepped between them, grasped Raven's arm and forced her to look at him. 'Your wagon — where is it?'

'Hoffman's livery stable.'

'Then do me a favor: take your horse there; have the hostler hitch him and your other horse to the wagon. Then wait for us.'

'Why, where're you and Momma going?'

'We'll be along.'

'When?'

'When we've a mind to. Now go.'

Raven didn't move.

'Trust,' Lawless reminded her. 'It's a notion you can live by.'

'Tell that to Pa,' she snapped. 'He trusted everybody and look what happened to him.' Turning, she hurried away.

Ingrid watched as her daughter mounted and rode off up the street. Then, too exhausted to cry, she wearily shook her head. 'What *am* I going to with her, Ben?'

'Be patient.'

'Now you sound like Sven.'

'She'll come around.'

'I used to think so,' Ingrid said dejectedly. 'Now I'm not so sure.'

'She will. Believe me.'

She looked at him, as if seeing him for the first time. 'I do believe you, Ben. I believe you and I believe *in* you. I want you to know that. I'd also like you to know how grateful I am for all you've done for us. Without you, I — '

He pressed his finger against her lips, silencing her.

Ingrid smiled, almost shyly, her blue eyes shiny with tears.

Behind them, on the street, riders clip-clopped past, wagons went creaking by . . . a rinky-dink saloon piano could be heard playing farther up the block.

Ingrid gazed wistfully after Raven, now dismounting outside the livery stable. 'I know at times it doesn't seem like it,' she said, 'but I love her so very much.'

Lawless, sensing she was thinking aloud, kept silent.

'That's what makes it so difficult, so painful . . . I love her but I can't seem to reach her . . . understand her . . . God knows I try, I really do. But she's so unpredictable. Most of the time, I don't even know what she's thinking. I mean, she can be so sweet one second, so hateful the next. And there doesn't seem to be any way of pinpointing what triggered the change. Not even her father, whom she adored and confided in, could always predict when it was going to happen. Difference is — was — he was so good-natured he was able to handle her mood swings better than me — which saved a lot of arguments.' She sighed, frustrated, then added, 'But now, with Sven gone, there'll be no buffer between Raven and me . . . no peacemaker . . . and without him there to pull us apart, heaven only knows what it'll come to.'

Sensing her despair, Lawless said, 'If it'll help, I don't need to push on right away.'

She turned, face uplifted to him. 'You don't?'

'No, ma'am.'

'But I thought . . . I mean, what about Arizona?'

'It'll always be there.'

'So will Stadtlander,' she reminded. 'He's not likely to quit trying to drive us out . . . especially after the way you treated him.'

'Let me worry about Stadtlander,' Lawless said. 'Just tell me if you want me to stay or not.'

‘’Course I want you to stay. My goodness, having you around — even for a little while — would be an enormous help.’

‘Reckon it’s settled then.’ Taking her arm, he led her down the courthouse steps.

At the bottom, she stopped and looked at him questioningly.

‘What?’ he said.

‘I was just thinking.’

‘About what?’

‘It’s a terrible thing to say, I know, but — ’

‘Tell me.’

‘I was thinking how lucky I am that Joey shot your horse.’

BOOK THREE

24

The next morning Sven was buried in a plain pinewood coffin on a low rise behind the barn. Ingrid chose the burial site. She'd often seen her husband standing there at sunset, silhouetted against the flaming sky as he stared across the flat open scrubland at the hills and, beyond, the distant mountains. Her husband loved mountains, she said, because they reminded him of his childhood home in Norway.

The funeral was a worthy tribute to Sven's way of life. Everyone from miles around showed up to pay their last respects. Among the grievers were several Mescaleros whom Sven had befriended over the years. Almighty Sky was not with them. But the old shaman had given one of his braves a feather from the wing of a golden eagle that Lolotea had blessed, saying it would help Sven's soul fly into the arms of the Great Spirit. 'He say to tell you,' the brave told Lawless, 'that you alone must place the feather on his coffin.'

'This I will do,' Lawless said. 'And when you next see Almighty Sky, tell him I am honored by this privilege.'

It was a simple ceremony. Father Blevins, an old, passionate, almost-blind minister at the Presbyterian Church in Santa Rosa, read a passage from Genesis and spoke of Sven's honesty, integrity and gentle, compassionate ways. 'This is a good man, Lord. He did not steal. He did not lie. He did not cheat. He led life as life should be led — as the Good Book instructed. And though he will be sadly missed by his beloved family and his friends, we must comfort ourselves with the knowledge that Our Lord has welcomed Sven Bjorkman into the Kingdom of Heaven where he will always smile down upon us. Amen.'

'Amen . . .' everyone murmured.

Father Blevins now beckoned to Lawless who stepped forward, knelt beside the open grave and placed the eagle feather atop Sven's coffin. 'Fly well, my friend,' he said. He then moved back so Ingrid and Raven could each throw a handful of dirt on the coffin and offer up their prayers. Both were still numb with grief and could barely get the words out.

Violet and Joey were equally devastated. They had known Sven for years. He and their father had often played chess together. And after their father was killed, they occasionally rode over to the ranch to spend the day with the Bjorkman family. It was good medicine. Though neither of them ever mentioned it, not even to each other, they found great comfort in being close to Sven.

But now Sven was gone, killed by a bullet like their father, and as Joey stood between his sister and Lawless, listening to everyone singing 'Rock of Ages', he cried his heart out.

* * *

After the funeral, some of their neighbors stayed on and ate a pot-luck lunch on the picnic table in front of the house. In hushed, emotional voices they praised Sven for his kindness and generosity. In some way, large or small, he had touched all of them. And now that he was dead, they assured Ingrid that if she or Raven or Violet and Joey ever needed help, all they had to do was ask and their needs would be taken care of immediately.

Grateful, Ingrid thanked everyone. She then explained that Violet and Joey had decided not to fight Stadtlander for their ranch but were going to telegraph their aunt and uncle in Denver, asking if they could live with them.

None of the neighbors wanted them to go; especially their closest neighbors, the Bartletts. 'You two leave now,' Mr Bartlett said, 'and it'll only fuel Stadtlander's greed. It's always been his dream to own all the land 'tween the Rio Grande and Deming. And now, having chased you and Joey off, he'll only try harder to gobble up our spreads as well.'

'I'm sorry,' Violet said. 'I hate to let you down, Mr Bartlett, but there's no reason for us to stay now. We've lost our home and, according to Mr Lawless, Mr Stadtlander's got all the lawyers in Deming spooked . . . and most likely everywhere else, too. On top of that he controls all the judges, so what chance would we have in court?'

'Reckon it would be too late even if you did hire a lawyer,' Mr McNally said glumly. 'I hear Stadtlander's already got geologists and miners digging for copper in Greenwater Canyon.'

A pall settled over the picnic table. No one even bothered to flick the flies away from the food.

Then suddenly Mr Bartlett banged his fist on the table, rattling plates and silverware. 'Dammit, quit acting like a bunch of quitters,' he yelled. 'We ain't sodbusters or squatters. We bought our land fair and legal.'

'And we may lose it the same way,' Mr Idlebauch said.

'Not me,' said Mr Bartlett. 'I'll die afore I let anyone steal our ranch.'

'That's mighty brave talk, Roy,' Mrs Deutsch said. 'But just how are you and your sons going to fight off twenty or thirty armed men?'

'Same way we fought off Apaches ten years ago — with lead.' He turned to Lawless, who hadn't spoken since lunch began, and said, 'Joey says you're the best he's ever seen with a gun. You willing to throw in with us against Stadtlander?'

'You've no right to involve Ben in our problems,' Ingrid said before Lawless could answer. 'This isn't his fight. He doesn't live here. Doesn't even have a stake in what's happened. Why should he risk his life for us? His future's in Arizona.'

'Maybe so,' Mr Bartlett said stubbornly. 'But I'm asking him just the same. And I'd like your answer,' he added to Lawless.

Lawless looked at the hardy, weathered faces looking expectantly at him around the table. They were the faces of pioneers, settlers, men and woman who had faced savage Indians, death, and ungodly conditions in wagon trains rolling through untamed country without complaint. They had survived against impossible odds and Lawless admired their courage and resourcefulness. He knew that without them most of the South-west would be nothing but wasteland and lawlessness. But he, too, was a survivor and he had no intention of fighting for them. Turning to Mr Bartlett, he said: 'I don't know what else Joey told you about me, but if he gave you the impression that my gun's for hire, he misled you. I'm a wrangler, not a shootist.'

'Then you won't help us?'

'No.'

Mr Bartlett sighed, resigned to his fate, and turned to his wife. 'It's getting late, Mother,' he said. 'Time we headed home.'

25

Lawless loaded the heavy trunk on to the wagon, wiped the sweat from his face with his sleeve and climbed on to the box-seat next to Ingrid and Raven. Two weeks had passed since Sven's burial and this morning he was driving the Morgans to the station at Santa Rosa so they could catch a train to San Francisco and from there a connection to Denver, where they would be met by their aunt and uncle.

'Now you're sure you've got everything,' Ingrid said to Violet and Joey who sat in back with their belongings. 'We don't want to get halfway there and have to turn back because you've forgotten something. You'll miss your train.'

'How could we forget anything?' Joey grumbled. 'Most everything we owned went up in smoke.'

'Quit talking like that!' Violet snapped. 'I told you before. Thanks to Aunt Sara and Uncle Dill, we got a chance to start over. We're going to live in a fine big house, a much finer and bigger house than we had here, with people who love us. You should be grateful, not complaining.'

'If they love us,' Joey said, 'why'd they take so long to answer your wire? It only takes a few seconds to get there.'

Ingrid had wondered the same thing but she refused to let herself or the Morgans dwell on it. 'That's only to the telegraph operator,' she said. 'Who knows how long it took after that. Denver's a big town and your aunt and uncle may live a long way from the office.'

'They got horses there, don't they?' Raven said.

'Of course they have horses,' her mother said. 'What's that got to do with it?'

'Everything. I never been to Denver, but I bet it don't take more a day at most to ride to the other side of town. That means it took twelve days for them to decide if they loved Vi and Joey enough to invite them to stay.'

'Raven's right,' Joey said to his sister. 'I told you before. They hate us. They've always hated us.'

'Nonsense,' Ingrid said. 'Your family is very close and very loving. I've heard your father say so, many times. Besides,' she added, giving Raven a 'be quiet' look, 'it snows in Denver. Very heavily, I've read. And sometimes for days at a time.'

'That's right,' Violet said. 'Aunt Sara once sent Pa a letter saying they'd been snowed-in for more than two weeks.'

'Which means she and your Uncle Dill decided they wanted you with them almost right away.'

That seemed to placate Joey. He leaned back against the trunk, pulled his cap down to shield his eyes from the sun and dozed off.

The wagon rolled on.

After a mile or so, Raven peered

around her mother at Lawless. 'Ever been to Denver?'

'Nope. Never have.'

'Then you don't know if it snows there in summer?'

It was summer now and Lawless frowned, wondering why Raven was determined to upset Joey. 'I do as a matter of fact. A fella I know, who grew up in the goldfields north of Sacramento, told me that Denver was so high in the mountains it snowed there all year round.'

Raven sighed, disappointed, and fell silent.

The next time she spoke, they had reached the train station on the outskirts of Santa Rosa and Lawless was unloading Violet and Joey's belongings. He'd thought he was alone, Ingrid having gone into the station house with Violet and Joey to buy their tickets to Denver via San Francisco. But then Raven peered around the side of the wagon at him, saying: 'This fella you once knew — what's his name?'

'That's my business,' Lawless said.
'I knew it!' Raven said triumphantly. 'There ain't no such fella. You just made him up to make Joey feel better.'
'No,' Lawless said. 'He exists all right.'
'Then why won't you tell me his name?'
'Why'd you want Joey to feel like he wasn't wanted?'
''Cause he made me kiss him once and I've hated him ever since.'
'Some girls would be flattered that he wanted to kiss them at all.'
'Well, I ain't some girls. Now,' Raven added, 'you going to tell me that fella's name or not?' When he didn't answer, she said disgustedly, 'Grownups! You're all the same. You want me to trust you, but when it comes time for you to trust me, oh no, that's a different kettle of stew.'
Lawless knew he was pinned. Resting his boot atop one of boxes, he gave Raven a long hard look and said, 'His name is Moonlight. Gabriel Moonlight.'
''Mean the shootist who works for

Mr Stadtlander?'

'The same.'

Raven gaped, eyes saucers. 'Goshaw-mighty, when'd you meet him?'

'A long time ago. His father was a Bible thumper in the gold camps. Gabe got tired of listening to the gospel and ran off when he was about fourteen or fifteen. He was fast with a gun even then and from what he told me, always on the prod. Getting into trouble all the time kept him on the run and eventually, after doing two years in Yuma Prison, he ended up here and went to work for Stadtlander.'

'And you'n him and Latigo all rode together?'

'For a spell, yeah. But that was a long time ago. I haven't seen Gabe for years.' He could have added that Will Lawless also rode with them but he didn't. He knew just the mention of his outlaw cousin would stir up questions he wasn't willing to answer.

Raven whistled, impressed. 'Latigo Rawlins and Gabriel Moonlight —

Sweet Mary, I sure would've liked to have seen people's faces when you three rode into town.' She waited, hoping he'd tell her some exciting stories. When he didn't, she added, 'Can I ask you one more question?'

'Can ask. Don't say I'll answer it.'

'How come they're still gunfighters on the prod and you ain't?'

Lawless shrugged. 'Life's a matter of choices, sprout. I didn't always make the right ones . . . then this happened.' He pulled down his shirt collar, revealing the top of his scar. 'Nothing like getting hanged to change your way of thinking. Figured I was living on borrowed time and been riding clean ever since. Now' — he ruffled her shiny black hair fondly — 'quit yapping and help me carry these boxes to the station.'

* * *

The train came and went, taking Violet and Joey with it. Ingrid shed a few tears, which seemed to irritate Raven, but managed to collect herself by the time she, Raven and Lawless had walked back to the wagon.

There, in the shade of the station house, three men stood waiting for Lawless. Two were deputies holding 10-gauge shotguns, the other, Sheriff Thorpe, was smiling like he'd been dealt a royal flush.

'Guess you didn't take my warning serious,' he said to Lawless. 'Well, so be it. You're under arrest.'

'For what?'

'Take your pick.' The sheriff held up a wanted poster. The face printed on it resembled Lawless, but the name above it was: Will Lawless. Wanted for murder, robbery, kidnapping — $10,000 — Dead or Alive!

'That's not me,' Lawless said. 'That's my cousin, Will.'

The sheriff rolled his eyes. 'Sure it is . . . and I bet your uncle's John Wesley Hardin.' He laughed at his own joke and the deputies joined in.

'It's the truth,' said Ingrid. 'His first name is Ben, not Will. Ask around. Anybody who was at my husband's funeral will tell you.'

Momentarily deflated, Sheriff Thorpe refused to back down. 'Just 'cause he tells everyone his name's Ben, Mrs Bjorkman, don't mean his real name ain't Will. Lots of outlaws use aliases to keep one jump ahead of the law.'

'How about another lawman?' Lawless said. 'Would you believe his word?'

'Depends on the lawman.'

'Sheriff Tishman, over at Borega Springs.'

Sheriff Thorpe frowned, surprised. 'You know Buck Tishman?'

Lawless nodded.

'Then you must know who put him in office?'

'I can guess — Stillman Stadtlander.'

'Do you also know that Sheriff Tishman almost got his foot blowed off by — '

'Latigo Rawlins, yeah, I was there.'

'If you know that, mister, what makes

you think Sheriff Tishman would help you, a man who's caused him and his benefactor nothing but grief?'

'Telegraph him and find out,' Lawless said.

'I'll do that,' Sheriff Thorpe said. 'Meanwhile, unbuckle your gun-belt. You're going to jail.'

'You can't arrest him,' Ingrid protested. 'Ben's innocent.'

'Not according to this poster, Mrs Bjorkman.'

'It's OK,' Lawless assured her. 'Sheriff Tishman will straighten things out. Here' — he unbuckled his gunbelt and handed it to her — 'keep this for me.' Before she could argue, he locked his hands behind his head and surrendered to the two deputies.

Sheriff Thorpe tipped his hat to Ingrid, then he and the deputies escorted Lawless into town.

26

It was stiflingly hot in the cell. Even the buzzing flies seemed sluggish in the unrelenting heat.

Noon melted into late afternoon. Sunlight still poured in through the tiny barred window forming shadowy stripes on the opposite adobe wall.

Lawless lay on the hard wooden cot, his buttoned, sweat-soaked shirt clinging to his skin, calmly smoking and trying to ignore the heat and the flies as he wondered how long it would be before Sheriff Tishman arrived. Having made the ride himself he knew it was less than forty miles to Borega Springs. Even in the relentless summer heat it shouldn't take the lawman more than two days to reach Santa Rosa.

That's if he comes at all, a voice said in Lawless's mind. Of course he'll come, Lawless thought. Why wouldn't he? The sheriff owes me his life. He's obliged to come. I know that, the voice said, and I'm sure he will. All I'm asking is what if he doesn't? But he's got to. Yes, yes, I know he's got to, the voice said, but what if he doesn't? What if he decides he doesn't owe you a damned thing and never comes? What will you do then?

The answer arrived sooner than he expected. Lawless heard voices in the office and moments later, the door to the cells was unlocked and a man entered. Waiting for the deputy to lock the door behind him, the man then swaggered up to Lawless's cell and grinned through the bars at him.

'Well, if this ain't frosty treat,' he said. 'The great Will Lawless locked up like a rat in a cage.'

Lawless ignored him and went on smoking.

Slade Stadtlander tauntingly fanned his fingers back and forth across the bars. 'How's it feel knowing you're 'bout to get your neck stretched?'

Lawless exhaled a stream of smoke and watched it spiraling toward the ceiling. 'If Daddy sent you here to deliver a message, Sonny, spit it out and then scat. You're fouling up the air.'

'This message ain't from Pa,' Slade said, 'it's from Sheriff Tishman. 'Course, if you don't want to hear it . . . '

Lawless got up and came to the bars. 'Let me see it.'

Slade took out a slip of paper, unfolded it and pressed it against the bars so Lawless could read the message. Meanwhile he said mockingly, 'Big Buck sends his regrets . . . but seems his sister in El Paso's taken sick of a sudden and poor ol' Buck, why he's so worried about her he jumped right on a train and went to hold her hand.'

The actual telegraph message wasn't so elaborate. It read: SHERIFF TISHMAN GONE TO EL PASO STOP VISITING AILING SISTER STOP NO IDEA WHEN HE WILL RETURN STOP DEPUTY LONNIE DAVIS.

Lawless, remembering the sheriff

saying he had no brothers or sisters, guessed that Stadtlander was behind the lawman's hasty departure and felt an icy hand grip his stomach.

'What's the matter?' Slade taunted. 'Feel that noose tightening?'

'There're others who can vouch for me,' Lawless said. 'Men I once rode with.'

'Don't count on it, Mr Gunfighter. When it comes to standing up against my pa folks have a habit of losing their memories.'

'Not the men I'm thinking of.'

Slade smirked. 'Wouldn't be talking about Latigo Rawlins and Gabe Moonlight, would you? 'Cause if you are, I got more bad news for you. Both of them have left the territory. You don't believe me?' he added, as Lawless looked dubious. 'Then maybe this'll convince you: soon as Pa found out Rawlins had shot Buck Tishman in the foot at the Morgan place, he cut him loose. No one's seen Shorty since.'

'That still leaves Gabe. Your father

would never cut him loose. He loves him like a son.'

'Wrong again. Pa caught him dealing from the bottom of the deck the other night. Wasn't the first time, either. So Pa gave him the boot. 'Course, Gabe didn't take kindly to that after all these years and to pay Pa back, stole his favorite stallion, Brandy. Some of the boys are out looking for him right now.'

The icy hand in Lawless's stomach gripped even tighter.

'Get Sheriff Thorpe,' he said. 'I want to talk to him.'

'Be happy to.' Slade turned, took a step then looked back at Lawless. 'One last thing,' he said, gloating, 'Pa's going to fix it so I'm the one who whips the horse out from under you. Can't tell you how much I'm going to enjoy that.'

* * *

Ingrid was allowed to bring supper to Lawless that night. After checking her basket to make sure there wasn't a gun or a knife hidden under the food, the deputy ushered her into the cell area. One look at her pale, tight-lipped face and Lawless knew she'd heard he was slated to hang.

'It's all over town,' she said, as she passed the food through the bars. 'Raven and I are spending the night with our friends, the Melvins, and all day long customers in their store were talking about it. I tried to tell them that you weren't lying — that you really weren't the outlaw Will Lawless — but I'm afraid most of them didn't believe me. And even the few who did weren't willing to come forward and tell the sheriff.'

'You can't blame them,' Lawless said. 'They know what Stadtlander is capable of.'

'I do indeed,' said Ingrid. 'Mr Melvin has heard rumors that Mr Stadtlander plans to block any attempt I make to hire a geologist or contact a mining company to see who would finance the digging for copper in Greenwater

Canyon. Of course, I don't have the money to hire anyone anyway, but it does show you how ruthless he can be.'

Lawless nodded. 'I wish I knew someone who could help you,' he said wistfully. 'But the people of wealth I once knew lost everything during the Civil War.'

Ingrid eyed him curiously. 'Is that where you're from — the South?'

Lawless nodded and looked away, unwilling to discuss his past. Biting into a leg of cold fried chicken, he nodded approvingly. 'Mmmm, this is sure mighty tasty.'

'I don't know how you can eat at a time like this,' Ingrid said. 'I surely couldn't.'

'Yet you still brought me supper.'

'I was afraid the sheriff might not let me see you otherwise.'

'Why not? I haven't been convicted of anything yet. First there has to be a trial and — ' He paused as he saw her frown, then said: 'If you've heard something different, tell me.'

Ingrid hesitated, not sure if she should tell him. 'It was Raven, not me,' she said finally. 'She heard two deputies talking as they went into the Las Flores — '

'Cally Sage's cantina?'

'Yes. Do you know her?'

'Some,' he said guardedly. Then: 'What did the deputies say?'

'That Slade had told them you weren't going to live long enough for a trial.'

'What else?'

'I don't know. Raven didn't hear anymore. By then, they had gone inside.'

Lawless dropped the half-eaten chicken leg into the basket and wiped the grease from his mouth and fingers. 'Reckon it's time I got out of here.'

'How can I help?' Ingrid asked.

'You can't.'

'Why not? You stood up to Stadtlander for us when you didn't have to — '

'That's different. I don't have a

daughter to look after. Ingrid,' he added as she started to protest, 'I appreciate the offer. But there's no way in hell I'm letting you get involved in this.'

'Dammit, Ben, I'm already involved. Or have you forgotten I just buried my husband?'

'I haven't forgotten anything,' Lawless said grimly. 'But Sven was the only friend I ever had. And I'll gladly hang before I let his wife risk going to jail for helping me escape.'

Ingrid sighed and shook her head. 'I should have listened to Raven. She said that's what you'd say. Guess she knows you better than I do.'

'Maybe one day, when enough time's passed, we can change that,' Lawless said.

He waited for her to answer, to offer him words of hope. But she just stood there, hands gripping the bars, lost in thought. Finally she said, 'That's very sweet of you, Ben. But I doubt if I'll ever care for another man again. Not the way I cared for Sven.'

'I wouldn't expect you to,' Lawless said. 'No man can take another man's place. Nor should he want to. His needs are different, his hopes are different . . . his love is different. All he can do is love a woman his way and hope that she will love him for his differences.'

Ingrid smiled, touched. 'You should've been a poet, Ben. That was beautiful.'

'I just wanted you to know how I feel, that's all.' He gently pressed his hands over hers. For the second time since he'd met her, it felt like he was holding sunshine.

For a moment Ingrid seemed to feel the same way. Then, as if afraid of her own feelings, she withdrew her hands, said: 'I'm sorry, Ben. It's too soon.'

Before Lawless could reply, a key turned in the lock and the deputy looked in. 'Time's up, Mrs Bjorkman. Sheriff said I was to only let you stay for ten minutes and — '

'It's all right, Deputy, I'm just leaving.' Ingrid turned to Lawless. 'Goodbye.'

He nodded goodbye. Then, as she reached the door, 'Ingrid.'

'Yes?'

'I'm a patient man.'

She gave him a quick, sad smile and left.

27

It was after midnight. The stores were closed, the streets almost empty. Except for the rowdies whooping it up in the Copper Palace and the Las Flores, everything was quiet in Santa Rosa.

Lawless lay on his cot in the cell, unable to sleep, a desert wind blowing in through the barred window refreshingly cool on his face.

Presently, he heard the door in the adjoining office open. Boots stomped in from outside. Voices and laughter followed. He guessed it was Deputies Lacey and McGowan returning from their last patrol around town. He listened intently. Shortly, he heard the higher-pitched voice of Lacey say goodnight; then a brief silence; then Deputy McGowan closing the front door and sliding the bolt into place. His boots clumped across the plank flooring. A key unlocked the door to the cells. Lawless closed his eyes and pretended to be asleep as the deputy looked in.

Satisfied all was well, Deputy McGowan locked the door. Lawless heard him cross to the stove, pour himself a cup of coffee and flop in the chair behind the sheriff's desk. Lawless smiled. McGowan enjoyed ordering folks around and Lawless guessed by now he had his boots up on the desk and was imagining how it would feel to be sheriff. A long silence followed. Lawless wondered if the deputy had dozed off. If he had, now was as good a time as any to try to break out.

Rising, Lawless quietly slid the cot over to the window, stood on it and peered out through the bars. There was a dirt alley running between the back of the jail and a large adobe-brick building that he guessed was some kind of storehouse. He tested the bars. They were buried in the lower and upper walls of the window and when he tugged on them, they didn't budge.

Even if he had a knife he doubted if he could dig them loose by morning.

Stepping down, he slid the cot back against the wall and checked the lock in the cell door. It was a large, uncomplicated lock stamped with the manufacturer's name: Sargent & Greenleaf. Lawless remembered the key was big and fitted so snugly Sheriff Thorpe had had trouble inserting it and removing it when he first locked Lawless up. The key also grated when it turned, suggesting the lock might be rusted inside. Still, Lawless thought, it was worth a try. Removing his belt, he held the buckle flat and inserted the metal prong into the lock. He gently twisted it around. It snagged against the mechanism, but was not stout enough to turn anything. After several tries, Lawless gave up and slipped the belt back through the loops on his jeans.

Escape was hopeless, he knew, unless he could trick the deputy into moving close enough to the bars so Lawless could grab him. But Deputy McGowan, though young and cocky, was no fool. In the few times he had entered the cell room, he had never come within arms' length of the bars.

Glum, Lawless sat on his cot, took out the makings and built a smoke. Striking the match on the wall he held it up for a moment, using the flame to illuminate his surroundings. Nothing but bars, walls, stone floor and a flat adobe ceiling that was out of reach and probably several feet thick. Frustrated, Lawless lit his cigarette from the sputtering flame and leaned back against the wall.

After all that life had thrown at him, he wondered, could he now really be doomed to hang — a second time? Was fate really that heartless? And what about the citizens of Santa Rosa — would they actually stand by and say nothing while an innocent man was hanged? If Stadtlander had anything to say about it, the answer was most definitely yes.

Damn, Lawless thought. If only Joey hadn't shot his horse, he'd be in

Arizona by now and —

Voices interrupted his thinking. Someone outside on the boardwalk was talking through the front door to the deputy. Lawless couldn't make out everything that was being said but he recognized the speaker's voice. It was Deputy James Lacey's and it sounded like he was asking McGowan to open the door.

'Goddammit, Jim,' Lawless heard Deputy McGowan reply, 'what in tarnation did you forget this time?'

Rising, Lawless went to the bars and listened. He heard McGowan's boots clumping to the door, then the scrape of the bolt being slid back — then the door opening — then a moment of silence followed immediately by the sound of a brief scuffle — and finally two bodies collapsing on the floor.

Before Lawless could figure out what was happening, a key unlocked the door to the cells. A man stepped in, a man who except for a full black beard and the trail dust caking his clothes, could have been Lawless's double.

'Well, if it ain't my favorite cousin,' Will Lawless said. He stepped close to the bars, whiskey fouling his breath, and grinned at Ben Lawless. 'Surprised to see me?'

'That's one way of putting it,' Lawless said grimly.

'My, my, sounds like you're still holding a grudge, *hombre*.'

'Not so long as you're holding those keys.'

Will chuckled, 'You always did know which side your biscuit was buttered on,' and unlocked the cell.

'Around you I had to,' Lawless said, adding: 'How'd you know I was here?'

'I told him,' a man said from the doorway. Dark-haired and bronzed by the sun, Gabriel Moonlight was even taller than Lawless and had the kind of ice-blue eyes that pierced right through to a person's soul. 'Cally told me yesterday at the hideout and I got word to Will, here. Figured since you were kin, he might want to help us cheat

Stadtlander out of a hanging.'

'Thanks, Gabe. I owe you,' Lawless said.

'C'mon, you jabbernuts,' someone yelled from the office. 'Hurry it up. The horses are falling asleep!'

'Christawmighty,' said Lawless, recognizing the voice. 'Just like old times.'

The three of them pushed out into the office where two bodies lay sprawled on the floor. One was Deputy Lacey. By the unnatural way his head was turned Lawless knew his neck was broken. The other man, Deputy McGowan, was unconscious and had blood seeping from two gashes on his temple.

Perched on the desk beside him, his dangling legs too short to reach the floor, was Latigo Rawlins. The dapper little gunman winked at Lawless and then pointed his carbine at Deputy McGown. 'Dumb bastard started coming around, so I had to give him another tap.'

'Better tie him up,' Gabriel said, 'or

we'll have a posse breathing down our necks.'

'Why waste good rope?' Will Lawless said. Before they could stop him, he whipped out a boot knife and sliced the unconscious deputy's throat. 'Reckon now we got all the time we need.'

'Goddamn you!' Lawless raged. 'Now I'm on the hook for two killings.'

'What of it?' Will said. 'They was going to hang you anyways.' Wiping his knife clean on the deputy's shirt, he stuck it in his boot and walked out.

'Ain't he a daisy?' Latigo said.

'I should've let the bastard drown,' Lawless said grimly. Then, as the others looked at him questioningly, 'When we were growing up, we were always fighting and one day he tried to push me down his old man's well. Will was stronger than me, but I was quicker. I wrestled loose and hit him. He went stumbling back, lost his balance and next thing I knew he'd fallen into the well.'

'And you were bone-headed enough

to pull him out?'

Lawless shrugged. 'He was my cousin.'

'What of it?' Latigo said coldly. 'Just 'cause you're kin don't mean you can't kill each other.'

'So you would've let him drown?'

'Not me,' Latigo said. 'I would've shot the sonofabitch as he was swimming around.' Jumping off the desk, he carefully stepped over the corpses and walked out.

Gabriel Moonlight shook his head in disgust. 'And goodness and mercy shall follow them for the rest of their lives.'

'Amen,' Lawless said. They left, closing the door behind them.

28

On their way to the border they stopped at the Bjorkman ranch to pick up Lawless's gun.

Despite the late hour a light glowed in the window. Guessing Ingrid was up for some reason and not wanting her anywhere near his cousin, Lawless reined up outside the gate and told Gabriel, Will and Latigo to wait for him. Dismounting, he handed the reins to Gabriel.

Instantly he had to jump back as the irascible all-black Morgan tried to bite him.

'When you going to teach that damn horse some manners?' Lawless cursed.

'I've tried teaching him,' Gabriel said. 'Sonuvagun's too mule-headed to learn.'

'Maybe you should've stoled another horse,' Will said.

'I didn't steal Brandy,' Gabriel said. 'I keep telling you that. I won him fair and square, aces and eights.'

'Yeah, but I heard you dealt yourself the second ace from the bottom of the deck.'

'That's a damn lie — and everyone at the table knows it.'

'Then how come Stadtlander's got men out looking for you?'

''Cause the old man can't stand losing — at anything.'

'If we're going to cross the border afore sunup,' Latigo reminded them, 'we best make tracks.'

'Be right back,' Lawless said. He ducked between the bars of the gate and hurried to the house. No one answered his first knock. He knocked again, slightly louder.

'Who is it?' Ingrid asked.

'Ben — open up.'

The door opened and Ingrid, framed by lamplight, stared at him in shock.

'I don't have time to explain,' Lawless said, 'but I need my gun.'

She reached behind the door and handed him his gunbelt. Looking tired and close to defeat, she asked him if he was all right.

He nodded. 'You're going to hear a lot of ugly stories about me tomorrow — about how I killed two deputies while breaking out of jail.'

'Nonsense!' She shivered despite the robe pulled tightly around her. 'You're many things, Ben, but I'll never believe you're a murderer.'

'What you believe won't matter. Not once they find the bodies. But I wanted you to hear the truth from me: I did not kill them.'

'I would've gone to my grave believing that anyway. But I'm still glad you told me.'

In the darkness beyond the gate a horse whinnied and stamped its hoof impatiently on the ground.

Ingrid looked questioningly at Lawless.

'Some men I'm with,' he said.

'If they need to water their horses — '

'No. I don't want you to see them or know who they are. That way, you don't have to lie when the sheriff questions you.'

'I thank you for that.'

'You're up late?'

'I couldn't sleep.'

'If it'll help . . . I'll stay a while.'

'Goodness no! This will be the first place they look.' She managed a tight thin smile. 'I'll be all right. Promise.'

'Sure you will. Just takes time is all.'

She looked off at the darkness, said distantly, 'It's not . . . I mean I'm not really afraid . . . though Raven says I am . . . it's just . . . all so new . . . you know, being alone . . . the two of us . . . out here . . . without Sven or, or you to . . . to . . . well . . . it can be a little unsettling.'

One of the men whistled.

'You'd better go,' she said.

Lawless nodded but didn't move.

'Will I ever see you again?'

'Of course,' he lied. 'Might be a spell, but . . . '

Ingrid nodded, understanding. 'I'll miss you.'

'Just don't forget me.'

'Do you really think I could?'

'I'll never forget you. Any of you.'

Ingrid smiled sadly. 'Life,' she said, 'why does it have to be so complicated?'

A second whistle, more impatient than the first, pierced the darkness.

'Take care of yourself, Ben.'

'You do the same.'

'I will.'

He wanted to say more, to tell her how he really felt about her, how that being with her and Sven and Raven was the best thing that had ever happened to him, but couldn't find the words.

Sensing his struggle, she leaned close and kissed his cheek. 'God speed, Ben Lawless.'

The urge to hold her, to feel her warm and soft and comforting against him was overwhelming. But he restrained himself, touched his hat and forced himself to walk away.

Never had he felt as empty.

Suddenly a slim boyish figure in a flannel nightgown pushed past her mother and caught up to Lawless.

'I trusted you,' Raven said angrily, 'and you weren't even going to say goodbye.'

He gathered her up, lifting her off her feet, and bear-hugged her. 'I wanted to, sprout. But I didn't have the guts.'

'Hah! You expect me to believe that?'

'Why would I lie?'

''Cause it's what grownups do when they let you down.'

'Trust . . . ' he reminded. 'It's a — '

'I know, I know,' Raven grumbled, ''a notion you can live by'.'

'And build on. Always remember that.'

She sighed. He felt her relax as her anger faded.

'All right,' she said grudgingly, 'I believe you. So, there.'

Pleased, he set her down.

She stood there in the darkness, looking up at him with her large, black, expressive eyes. 'I love you,' she said.

He smiled, knowing he felt the same way about her.

'Ain't you going to say you love me?'

'You already know that.'

'Then say it. Say: I love you.'

'Damn, if you aren't the pushiest girl I ever met.'

'Only when I want something and right now I want you to say you love me.'

'God help me and the men that come after me,' Lawless said. He hunkered down and looked deep into her shining eyes. 'I love you, sprout. I always will.' The words sounded strange coming out of his mouth but he knew he meant them. Kissing her on the forehead, he spun her around and gave her a gentle push in the direction of the house. 'Look after your mother for me. She's going to need you.'

He turned toward the gate and walked off into the darkness.

Behind him he heard Raven say, 'I told him I loved him, Momma.'

'I know, sweetheart. I heard you.'

'Said he loved me back.'
'Yes, I know.'
'You love him too, don't you?'
'Yes,' Ingrid said.
'Like you loved Pa?'
'No, sweetheart. Not like that. But in a very special way.'

29

It was shortly before sunup when the four of them crossed the border into Mexico. They crossed where there was no fence, only endless miles of pale lemony scrubland and rocks, and rode westward toward Las Palomas.

There was no moon but plenty of coyotes. They sang in mournful chorus all around them.

'Once, when I was holed up in the Mimbres,' Gabriel said as they followed Will into a sandy gully, 'I ate nothing but coyote meat for three weeks.'

'What'd it taste like?' Latigo asked.

'Dog. Only tougher . . . stringier.'

'You've ate dog?'

'Uh-uh.'

'Then how do you know what it tastes like?'

' 'Paches told me. They eat dog all the time.'

' 'Paches'll eat anything,' Will said disgustedly, 'just so it's breathing and sometimes even if it ain't. Makes no matter to them.'

No one said anything.

They rode on in the cool darkness. They were deep in the gully now and on both sides of them the steep, rock-strewn banks rose up like small cliffs. It was the perfect place for an ambush and to a man, they were glad it wasn't ten years ago or behind each rock would have been an Apache.

'How come you were holed up so long?' Lawless asked Gabriel.

'Posse was hunting me for robbing a cantina.'

'A *cantina*? Jesus, you must've been pretty desperate.'

'I was drunk as a skunk is what I was. Anyways, the posse wasn't after me for the money — hell, I only got seven dollars. It was on account of I accidentally shot the ear off the Mex who owned the place and the sheriff, damn his hide, was sweet on his daughter.' He paused as the others started laughing, then added, 'As if that weren't enough incentive, happens there was also a reward out for me . . . and the mayor was looking to get himself re-elected. I tell you, for a spell there it seemed like all of New Mexico was beating the bushes for Mesquite Jennings.'

His companions doubled over with laughter.

They rode on around a bend. Ahead the gully widened and the rock-covered banks got steeper. Shortly, they passed a boulder shaped like a tombstone. Immediately Will, who was riding alongside Lawless, made sure no one was watching him. Then he gently tapped his horse with his spurs. The sorrel quickened its pace and moved a length ahead.

Not conscious of the fact that he was now riding alone, Lawless looked back at Gabriel and shook his head disparagingly. 'Mesquite Jennings,' he said. 'By God, I almost busted a gut laughing when I heard that's what you'd named yourself.'

'What's wrong with Mesquite Jennings?' Gabriel said.

'What's right with it, you mean.'

'Cally liked it.'

'You were bedding her, for Chris'sake, what the hell did you expect her to say?'

Gabriel looked hurt. 'Well, it was good enough for some dime novel writer to dream up.'

'What's that prove?' said Latigo.

'Could you write a book?'

'Never tried. I'll tell you this, though: if I ever did write one, I sure as sweet Texas wouldn't name my hero after a goddamn bush!'

Lawless started laughing again.

'Mesquite ain't a bush,' said Gabriel, 'it's a tree — '

A sudden volley of shots poured from the rocks on both sides of them. Will's horse screamed, staggered and went down, pitching him over its head.

Bullets whined all around them.

Lawless, Gabriel and Latigo jumped

from their mounts and dived behind the nearest rocks.

The shooting continued, heavier now.

Pinned down, the three could only get off occasional shots.

'Stadtlander?' Lawless said to Gabriel.

'I doubt it. We had strict orders never to cross over.'

'Well, it can't be a posse,' Latigo said. 'Not unless someone tipped off the sheriff 'bout busting you out.'

'Even if they did,' Lawless said, 'they wouldn't know where we were headed. We didn't know ourselves till after we crossed the border.'

Bullets steadily chipped at the rocks, ricocheting dangerously close.

'Who then?' said Gabriel.

Will came scrambling up, Winchester in hand. 'Goddamn bandidos! The wash is crawling with 'em.'

'*Bandidos* — with repeating rifles?'

'Why not? Enough pesos will buy you anything.'

'How many, y'think?'

'More'n we can handle,' said Gabriel.
'Not if we could get to our rifles.'
'First we got to get to our horses.'
They looked at each other, knowing whoever went was risking his life.
'I'll go,' said Will. 'Cover me.' He was gone, disappearing into the darkness before they could stop him.
The three exchanged surprised looks then straightened up and emptied their Colts into the enemy. It was still too dark to see if there were any hits. But a few painful cries followed by a body tumbling into the wash told them not every shot had missed.
'What do you make of it?' Lawless said as they ducked down and began reloading.
'Of what?' Latigo said.
'Will taking off like that. I mean when's the last time that bastard ever volunteered to get shot?'
' 'Cept he's not getting shot,' Gabriel said. 'And he ain't going for our horses either. See?' He pointed to a shadowy figure scrambling up the rocks on the

opposite bank of the gully. 'Son of a buck's heading right for where most of the shooting's coming from.'

The three looked at each other, puzzled. Then it hit Lawless.

'That mercenary sonofabitch! He sold us out.'

'How you figure that?' Latigo said.

'Who told us he knew of a hideout near Las Palomas?'

'Will.'

'Who said this gully led to a shortcut through the hills?'

'I see what you mean.'

'Damn his lying hide,' said Gabriel. 'We get out of here alive, I'll make sure he never back-stabs us again.'

It was growing light. A pale mauve wash began spreading across the gray sky as dawn broke beyond the mountains in the east.

They could now see across the gully. Peering between the rocks they caught a glimpse of Will Lawless. Almost to the top of the opposite bank, he ducked behind a rocky overhang and joined a group of his men who were hiding there. The incessant rifle fire that had kept Lawless, Latigo and Gabriel pinned down abruptly ceased. They leaned back against the rocks and began reloading.

'How much you figure Stadtlander's paying Will to kill both of us?' Gabriel asked Lawless.

'As much as it takes.'

'So it ain't going to end here, no matter what?'

'No matter what.'

Gabriel shook his head in disgust. 'All these years I thought I knew that old man. He took me in, treated me fair, made me ramrod — even favored me over his own boy most of the time. Now he wants to kill me 'cause he lost one lousy hand at poker.'

'You can't put a price on pride, Gabe. We made a fool out of him and he's a mighty proud and vengeful man.'

'Whatever he's paying,' Latigo put in, 'you can bet your last dollar that he'd double it to get you back alive.'

'That'll never happen,' Gabriel said. 'I've seen some of his hangings. He don't use a knot to break your neck. Lets a fella just hang there, kicking and fighting for air, until he's dead. It ain't pretty.'

Lawless wasn't listening. 'You know what I can't figure out? If Will planned this, why'd they shoot his horse?'

'Ever knowed a greaser who was a good shot?' Gabriel said.

'They're not Mex. They're Will's men. I'd bet on it.'

'That'd explain the Winchesters,' Latigo said.

'Yeah, but not why they shot his horse.'

'You ask me,' Gabriel said, 'there's nothing to figure out. It was just a lousy shot.'

'Mean they were aiming at one of us?'

'Not us — you,' said Latigo.

'You were riding right behind him,' Gabriel reminded. 'And it's no secret he's never forgiven you for shooting his old man.'

'I had no choice,' Lawless said. 'Uncle Jesse was raging drunk and came at me with a scattergun. Will knows that. He was there, beside the cotton gin when it happened.'

There was a burst of rifle fire. Bullets ricocheted off the rocks around them, forcing them to hit the ground. When the shooting ceased, they heard Will call out, 'Lefty? Lefty, you hear me?'

'I hear you,' Latigo said.

'I ain't looking to kill you. You want to leave, get on your horse and ride out.'

'And if I don't?'

'We'll bury you feet up, same as Gabe and Ben.'

'I need to think on it,' Latigo said.

'Don't trust him,' Lawless said. 'You step out there and he'll gun you down just for the fun of it.'

'Tell me something I don't know,' Latigo said.

'This is your last chance, Lefty,' Will shouted after a long silence.

Latigo ignored him.

Colts fully loaded now, the three prepared to shoot it out.

'Something else that doesn't make sense,' Lawless said. 'If Will wants me dead so badly, why didn't he tell Stadtlander that you two were breaking me out? Then the sheriff and his deputies could've been waiting for us the moment we walked out of the jail. That way, Will would not have only gotten his blood money, but in a day or two, he'd have a front-row seat at my hanging.'

'He already tried that once,' Gabriel said without thinking. 'And look where it got him — '

'Shut up,' Latigo hissed.

But it was too late.

'What're you saying?' Lawless demanded. Then, when they didn't answer, 'Did Will have something to do with this?' He indicated the rope scar around his neck.

'Forget it,' Latigo said. 'That's yesterday's news.'

'You sons of bitches,' Lawless said.

'How long you known?'

''Bout a month after the hanging,' Gabriel said.

'We wanted to tell you,' Latigo said, 'but since you couldn't remember nothing, what was the point?'

'Tell me now,' Lawless said grimly.

'Will set you up,' Latigo said. 'He pistol-whipped two *rurales* to death then had one of his men tell their officer that Will Lawless was responsible and where they could find him. 'Course, he was leading them right to you. The *rurales* took the bait, mistook you for Will and . . .'

Lawless didn't hear any more. He didn't even hear the bullets whining and ricocheting all around them. In his mind the impenetrable darkness that had always blocked his memory of those missing twelve hours now melted away; and just like that, clear as day, he saw himself struggling to escape from the men holding him . . . and behind them more angry faces, Mexican faces, *rurales*, their high-crown sombreros pushed back off their heads, watching him being hoisted on to his horse and then the noose dangling in front of him, a hand now looping it around his neck and then, behind him, the officer whipping his horse . . . the animal lunging forward and . . .

. . . the ungodly horror of the rope jerking tight . . . crushing against jugular . . . choking him . . . and . . . then . . .

. . . the picture he was visualizing faded . . .

He tried desperately to get it back; to force his mind to show him what happened next, but it was useless. It was like staring into an empty black hole.

Now, as he crouched behind the rock, he saw Latigo and Gabriel returning the fire of their attackers.

'Reloading,' Gabriel sang out. He crouched down beside Lawless and began pulling cartridges from his gunbelt.

Lawless grabbed his arm. 'Gabe, you

got to tell me. What happened? Why aren't I dead? How'd I get away?'

'I don't know, Ben. If I did, I'd surely tell you.'

'What about Lefty?'

'He don't know either.'

Latigo fired his last round and ducked down beside them. Checking his gunbelt, he said, 'One more load and I'm out.'

'Two for me,' said Gabriel.

Lawless knew then what he had to do.

'Will!' he shouted. 'Will, this is Ben.'

'What do you want?'

'To talk.'

' 'Bout what?'

'You'n me. Settling scores.'

No answer.

'This is family doing. Between cousins. Why not end it that way?'

'Keep talking.'

'Tell your men to stop shooting. I'm coming out.'

'Alone?'

'Alone.'

'You heard him,' Will told his men. 'Hold your fire.'

'One last thing,' Lawless said. 'No matter who's left standing, Gabe and Lefty get to ride out of here.'

Silence.

'It's almost light,' Lawless continued. 'You might get us all in the end but not before one of us finds a way to kill you.'

Will looked at the ever-lightening mottled sky and knew Lawless was right.

'Deal,' he said.

The gully became deadly quiet.

'Are you loco?' Gabriel hissed at Lawless. 'You can't go out there. Like you just told Lefty, the bastard'll shoot you afore you cast a shadow.'

'Then I'll have to shoot him first.'

'Even if you do,' Latigo said, 'his men will blow you to pieces.'

'Eventually they will anyway.' Lawless indicated his empty gunbelt. 'All I got is what's in the chamber,' he spun the cylinder of his Colt.

'Then we'll all go together,' Gabriel said.

'Don't include me,' Latigo said. 'There's no profit in dying.'

Gabriel shot him a disgusted look then stood up.

'Thanks,' Lawless gripped his shoulder fondly, 'but this is something I have to do alone.'

'No profit in being noble either,' Latigo said.

Lawless ignored him. 'You can do me a favor, though,' he said to Gabriel.

'Name it.'

'Afterward, if he's still standing, I'll die happy if you shoot him.'

'Count on it,' said Gabriel.

'Watch the fingers on his gun-hand,' Latigo told Lawless. 'He flexes them just before he draws.'

Gabriel glanced at the coming dawn. 'You'll have to get close to see his fingers.'

'I intend to,' Lawless said. 'After all the goddamn grief he's caused me, I want to see his face as he dies.' Pulling his black, flat-crowned hat firmly down on his head, he squeezed out between the rocks and walked toward the middle of the gully.

'Whenever you're ready,' he called out.

Loose stones and dirt came slithering down as Will Lawless slowly descended the opposite bank.

Lawless turned and faced him.

It took a few moments but finally his cousin reached the floor of the gully and came toward him.

'Before we do this,' Lawless said as Will got close, 'I want to know something.'

'Make it short.'

'Why didn't the *rurales* finish the job? Why am I standing here wearing this souvenir?' He unbuttoned his shirt to show the rope scar.

Will grinned, showing broken, snuff-stained teeth. 'Mean you ain't figured that out yet?' Even as he spoke the fingers on his right hand flexed and he went for his gun.

Lawless did the same.

Two explosions, so close it was impossible to know who fired first.

But Lawless knew.

He knew even as Will's bullet punched him in the chest, knocking him back, his legs now buckling so that he fell to his knees.

Will holstered his iron and hunkered down in front of him.

Lawless looked at him through a red haze. His Colt slipped from his numb fingers . . . and fell to the ground.

'Why, Cousin,' Will said, 'I do believe I've done you in.'

Then, when Lawless didn't answer, 'It was the rope, Ben. It broke while you was hanging there.'

There was a dull roaring in Lawless's ears. He saw Will's lips moving in front of his face yet couldn't hear what he was saying.

' . . . and 'cause it was a brand new rope, never been used afore, the officer, being a fine Catholic and a right religious fella, figured it was an act of

God . . . that the Good Lord was telling him he shouldn't hang you. So he up'n let you go . . . '

Lawless never heard him. He fell forward on to his face, dead before he hit the sand.

Will straightened up and spat on Lawless. 'That's for Pa,' he said, adding, 'Hope you rot in Hell.'

'Will . . . '

Will Lawless spun around and saw Latigo standing before him.

'Try me,' the little gunman said.

'I got no quarrel with you, Lefty.'

'I'm going to kill you just the same.'

Knowing he meant it, Will reached for his gun.

The weapon never cleared leather.

Latigo's bullet tore through his chest, ripping a hole in his heart.

Will staggered, eyes saucers, crumpled, and fell lifelessly on his back.

Gabriel, after making sure Lawless was dead, joined Latigo. Together they faced the dozen or so renegades, most of them hardened, low-life border trash, descending from the rocks.

Gabriel spoke softly, barely moving his lips. 'First time I ever known you to kill someone for free.'

'Don't get used to it,' Latigo said.

'Wasn't figuring to. I mean how many miracles you get to see in your life?'

' 'Sides,' said Latigo, 'it wasn't exactly free. Will's worth five thousand dollars in New Mexico, dead or alive. If I've a mind to, I'll take his body back and collect it.'

'The reward,' Gabriel said. 'I'd forgotten all about that. Well, least now you've restored my faith in human nature.'

The renegades had reached the floor of the gully.

Gabriel and Latigo tensed, ready to shoot it out.

But the renegades had had enough. They continued on up the gully, soon disappearing around a bend where their horses awaited them.

Gabriel and Latigo waited until they heard them ride away before they returned to Lawless.

'If you was Ben,' Gabriel said, 'on which side of the border would you want to be buried?'

'Side I was born on,' Latigo said.

Together they lifted the corpse and carried it to Lawless' horse. There, they wrapped their dead friend in his bedroll, gently draped the body over the saddle and roped it tight.

'Sad day,' Gabriel said.

'They're all sad and getting sadder,' Latigo said, adding, 'You riding north with me?'

'Not unless you're anxious to see me hang.'

Latigo grinned. 'If I see Cally, want me to tell her where you are?'

'She already knows. But in case she's forgotten where I'm going to hole up, it's just south of — '

Latigo cut him off. 'Don't tell me, Gabe. That way I won't ever be tempted to hunt you down for the reward.'

Gabriel chuckled. 'Lefty,' he said, 'if I didn't know better, I'd say you was getting soft.'